"There Is A Limit On This Marriage."

"I know," Jeff replied. "Part of the deal is that neither of us will fall in love. I think that's a safe assumption. I'm not the marrying kind and you're not going to stay on my ranch. I'll tell you what, Holly, I'm never going to live in a city."

She gazed into his wide gray eyes and knew he meant every word, just as she did. "This is a doomed marriage," she said.

"Not doomed. Just exactly what we contracted it to be—temporary. One year only and then it's over. No strings, no heartbreak, because no one's heart is involved."

Something hurt deep inside her at his words. Was she having real feelings for her husband...the husband she wasn't allowed to love?

Dear Reader,

This is the second story involving twin billionaire brothers. *Tempting the Texas Tycoon* was the first book with Noah Brand. Now *Marrying the Lone Star Maverick* is the story of his identical twin, Jeff Brand, who is physically just like Noah, but in personality so different. Noah brings a woman into Jeff's life who is Jeff's opposite in everything. She loves cities, opera and shopping. Driven, Holly Lombard is an ambitious workaholic who takes life seriously. Jeff, on the other hand, is an easygoing, laid-back cowboy who loves the country and his horses and feels constricted by a city.

When these two are thrown together, a blaze ignites. How spicy is love when it attracts two opposing personalities? When they fall in love, trouble deepens for both. What kind of sacrifices will each have to make? The dynamics between the two protagonists constantly change. Against the backdrop of Texas—the Western ranch country with mesquite and cactus, the glittering city of Dallas, the lush green Hill Country—the story unfolds with the billionaire twins who compete yet band together when they need to help each other. Twins who are close and know each other as well as each knows himself. Here, now, is the second Texas twin's story.

Sara Orwig

SARA ORWIG

MARRYING THE LONE STAR MAVERICK

Silhouette®
Desire

Published by Silhouette Books
America's Publisher of Contemporary Romance

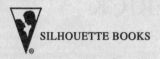

SILHOUETTE BOOKS

ISBN-13: 978-0-373-73010-0

MARRYING THE LONE STAR MAVERICK

Copyright © 2010 by Sara Orwig

Visit Silhouette Books at www.eHarlequin.com

Printed in U.S.A.

Books by Sara Orwig

Silhouette Desire

Falcon's Lair #938
The Bride's Choice #1019
A Baby for Mommy #1060
Babes in Arms #1094
*Her Torrid Temporary
   Marriage* #1125
The Consummate Cowboy #1164
*The Cowboy's Seductive
   Proposal* #1192
World's Most Eligible Texan #1346
Cowboy's Secret Child #1368
The Playboy Meets His Match #1438
Cowboy's Special Woman #1449
††*Do You Take This Enemy?* #1476
††*The Rancher, the Baby
   & the Nanny* #1486

Entangled with a Texan #1547
**Shut Up and Kiss Me* #1581
**Standing Outside the Fire* #1594
Estate Affair #1657
†*Pregnant with the First Heir* #1752
†*Revenge of the Second Son* #1757
†*Scandals from the Third Bride* #1762
Seduced by the Wealthy Playboy #1813
‡*Pregnant at the Wedding* #1864
‡*Seduced by the Enemy* #1875
‡*Wed to the Texan* #1887
**Dakota Daddy #1936
**Montana Mistress #1941
**Wyoming Wedding #1947
Tempting the Texas Tycoon #1989
Marrying the Lone Star Maverick #1997

††Stallion Pass
*Stallion Pass: Texas Knights
†The Wealthy Ransomes
‡Platinum Grooms
**Stetsons & CEOs

SARA ORWIG

lives in Oklahoma. She has a patient husband who will take her on research trips anywhere from big cities to old forts. She is an avid collector of Western history books. With a master's degree in English, Sara has written historical romance, mainstream fiction and contemporary romance. Books are beloved treasures that take Sara to magical worlds, and she loves both reading and writing them.

To David, Hannah, Rachel, Ellen,
Elisabeth, Colin, Cameron

Prologue

He'd never met a horse he couldn't break. The sleek sorrel had been a struggle, but now, under the bright lights of the corral, Jeff Brand felt the horse move smoothly at the merest touch. When he heard a car engine, he gave it little heed—the cowboys who worked for him often came and went at night.

"I thought that was you." Jeff reined the horse to the side at the sound of a familiar voice.

In chinos, loafers and a neat button-down plaid shirt, his twin brother, Noah, looked like what he was—a city guy. His slow climb over the fence only underscored that.

"Is Dad all right?" Jeff asked, holding his breath. Their father's second heart attack had scared the entire family. He was unable to imagine anything else could bring Noah to the ranch at this hour.

"Dad is okay. Didn't mean to startle you driving out here without calling. That's not why I'm here."

The horse pranced slightly and Jeff reined him in again. "So what does bring you out here at this time of the night?"

"I was afraid I wouldn't catch you during the day. As I recall, you always did spend a lot of nights riding. Great waste of evenings, if you ask me," he added, grinning at Jeff.

Jeff rode closer. His horse snorted and pranced a few steps away, fighting him for a moment before doing as Jeff wanted.

"New horse?"

"Yep. Past two owners couldn't quiet him down. I think he's going to be great."

"I think you might be right. He looks like a runner."

"He is. It always amazes me," Jeff said, pushing his wide-brimmed Stetson to the back of his head, "how you have an eye for horseflesh when you hate everything about the country."

"It's easy to explain. I like to win at the races and the one way to do that—" He swung his leg and jumped down.

"—is to know horses," Jeff finished. "Let me take care of him and you can tell me what it is you want. And I *know* you want something badly to drive all the way out here at this hour of the night."

"You're on target there. I'd rather be home with my wife and child than out here with you and a contrary horse."

Jeff took the reins and began walking toward the gate. "We can talk in the barn."

Inside, as Jeff unsaddled the sorrel, Noah sat on a stack of bales of hay.

"They think Dad can come home from the hospital the first of next week, but Dr. Gracy said he has to retire. Dad can't keep from worrying about business and getting uptight about deals, you know him."

"Damn, I hate to hear that. His job is his whole life," Jeff said, lifting the saddle off his horse. He left to get a bucket of water and returned in seconds. "Dad doesn't even have hobbies. There's nothing else in his life."

"It's difficult to imagine what's happened. Knox Brand and Brand Enterprises are synonymous. That's why I'm here. Dad's only staying on as chairman, but we're handling the Cabrera leather line now and we've taken on two other companies. I need help badly. Your help."

"Oh, hell no," Jeff said, as he glanced at his brother and saw the worried frown on Noah's face. He realized Noah was in earnest and his heart sank.

"Dammit, Noah, you know how I feel about the corporate life."

"Look, just do it for one year. Help me get someone else trained for this spot. I can't put someone new and green in it. You know the business from working there until you gave it up for ranching. You're on the board, so you keep up. You know me. You'll know what I want and what I don't. You know the financial side. You're a negotiator and a closer."

"I mean no." Jeff brushed his mount in long strokes. While he hated to say *no*, working in the Brand corporate headquarters would suck the life out of him.

"Your big objection was always Dad. He'll be gone."

"You're just like him, Noah."

"No, I'm not. Have I ever tried to run your life? You'd be a natural fit for the Cabrera line. It's only one year, Jeff," Noah said and Jeff knew he was in for a fight. When he wanted something, Noah was as stubborn as their dad. "I've got someone in mind we can move up later, but he's not ready at this point."

"That is twelve months too long," Jeff said patiently.

"All right," Noah said, walking around to lean on a stall as Jeff moved to the other side to brush down the sorrel. Jeff worked in silence while Noah marshaled his argument. "I'll up the ante." He sighed. "I'll get my assistant to help you. She knows that company as well as I do."

"That doesn't change my mind," Jeff replied.

"I just need you badly. Name what you want in return."

Jeff stopped brushing the horse and turned to stare at his brother. He had seen Noah in bad times, but before it had never been like this.

Rubbing the back of his neck, Jeff tried to think what would make the job palatable. "All right, Noah, I'll give you my terms. Plus a million up front for agreeing to do this, plus commissions if my division increases sales and on every acquisition I make. Oh, and I'll expect a salary like yours. I want to work part of the time from here. I'll put your assistant up."

"You don't want much, do you?" Noah snapped, sounding more like their father as his face flushed.

Jeff returned to brushing the horse. "Take it or leave it. You're the one who came to me."

"I might as well turn the company over to you," Noah grumbled. "Those are pricey demands. You don't even know what my salary is."

"I know it's good." Jeff continued taking care of his horse. If Noah accepted, hopefully Jeff could live with such a lucrative deal for the coming year.

"You drive a hard bargain, Jeff."

"That's why you want me to be your closer."

"I hate it when you're right. You get what you want. All right. I'll give you my assistant and you can work from your damn ranch. Work one day a week in the office. We'll set it up so you'll handle the Cabrera saddle and boot account from there, plus some others."

"I suggest you don't mention the terms of agreement to Dad. Don't want to give him another attack."

"That's cold. I thought the bad blood between you and Dad was improving. Anyway, I'm glad to have you, and I want you satisfied, too. This is good, Jeff. I can sleep nights now. I'll never understand why you left, because you have a mind for business."

"Versus spending my time with horses," Jeff said with a smile.

Noah shook his head.

"It boils down to I need your help. Understand that there'll be times you can't work from here. Most of the time you can. We can videoconference calls and meetings that have to include you."

"I don't see how you can possibly want me so badly."

When Jeff thought about what he'd asked for and how his fortune would grow, he had mixed feelings. Dread and reluctance filled him right along with anticipation and excitement because the promises were dazzling, especially coming on top of his ranch income and inherited money. One year wasn't forever. "You better need me as badly as you say. If I find out you don't, I'm gone, Noah."

"You'll see for yourself," Noah said. "Anything that isn't going well, just tell me. Can you start Monday? It would help this first week if you'd stay in the office. You can get the paperwork done to get you on the payroll."

Jeff wondered how the job would play out. "You've got yourself a deal," he said, questioning what he was getting himself into and how much it would change his life.

One

An hour before the office officially opened Monday morning, Holly Lombard smiled as she walked into Noah Brand's office. She'd been summoned to see him and she had a stack of papers, assuming he had questions about the new line they were introducing. She crossed his office, her footsteps silent on the thick Oriental carpet.

"Morning, Holly," Noah said, looking up from his desk. "Have a seat. I want to talk to you before everyone starts arriving."

"Congratulations," she said, sitting on a chair that was the finest leather Brand Enterprises carried. "I read your e-mail and saw that you got what you wanted."

"Thanks. Jeff starts today," Noah said, looking at her across his wide, antique mahogany desk, and she could hear the triumph in his tone of voice. "And that brings us to my purpose in talking to you. I have a proposition for you."

Surprised, she placed her stack of papers on the table beside her and waited.

"I made Jeff an offer that he accepted, but it's contingent on you taking a new position."

The first quiver of apprehension pricked her, but she dismissed it as ridiculous. "This is out of the blue," she said.

"I know, but I had to do some arm-twisting to get Jeff. He's excellent, Holly."

She reserved judgment. From Noah's conversations over the years, she knew his twin had walked out on Brand Enterprises a long time ago to become, over the years, a cowboy out on a West Texas ranch. She couldn't imagine that he could cope with the business.

"I want you to work with Jeff. In turn, I'll move you up from my assistant to Executive Western Marketing Manager and give you a twenty-percent pay raise. That's a big move, Holly. And you're young."

"Do I have a choice here?" she asked, appalled by the thought of working with Jeff Brand.

"Of course. I'm not going to lose you just because you won't accept. It's only a year. You'd get a jump in salary, title and responsibility. That's a career builder."

"I'd work for your brother, instead of you?" she repeated, thinking it would be death to her career. She'd leave the dynamic head of the corporation to work for a cowboy.

"That's correct. And I've told him he can work all but one day a week at his ranch."

"Oh, no!" she cried, jumping to her feet. "I'm not getting stuck out on a ranch in the middle of nowhere working for someone who has almost no business experience. I'm sorry, but I won't do it," she said, wondering if her career at Brand was going to end today. "I'm sorry, but that's absurd to even ask someone to do such a thing. It would kill my career." Hurt and furious that Noah would ask this of her, she drew herself up. "I can look for another job—would prefer to."

"Calm down and sit again," Noah said, sounding as if he were just telling her about a new design they were getting for one of their furniture lines. "Jeff may be a little rusty and needs to be brought up to speed, but you'll be pleasantly surprised. You can have a company car and all expenses paid. Look, I want Jeff and you're perfect to work with him. It'll be as good as if I was there to help him myself, which I can't do with Dad gone."

Noah rubbed his neck and she knew he was mulling over some bigger incentive. This was lousy thanks for all the work and success she'd had with the company.

"Any way you look at it, this is a demotion. You're sticking me in the boonies with an inexperienced cowboy. I loathe horses, country and Western stuff."

Noah shot her a look and she wondered if she'd overstepped her bounds, but it no longer mattered. Better her career crumbled before her eyes than she moved to the boonies. Noah waved his hand.

"Hold it, Holly." Noah did some figuring as he scribbled on a piece of paper. She sat, but wanted to pace the floor and scream at him. This was unfair and a huge waste of her talents. She wished Knox Brand were back on the job.

Noah came around his desk. "Here's the deal I'll make you. In addition to the raise and promotion, I'll pay you a bonus when you start and a bonus when you finish—$125,000 to start, $125,000 when the year is up."

With her stomach churning, Holly gazed out the window, knowing the offer had just become too lucrative to turn down without serious consideration. She envisioned West Texas—mesquite, cactus and dust. How out of touch could she get?

"You're not bowled over by my offer," Noah remarked dryly. "Make each payment $250,000, Holly."

Startled, she looked up at him. "That's a half-million-dollar bonus to do this. You want me in the worst way."

"Yes, I do. I told you, he's a negotiator and a financial whiz. He didn't make all of his fortune on cattle. I can count on him. He isn't an unknown. The two of you would be the best possible team. I won't worry about anything I turn over to you."

"I'm flattered by that endorsement," she remarked dryly. The amount he'd just offered dazzled her. "For that much money plus the promotions, Noah, I can put up with a lot. I'd work with a gorilla at the zoo," she said and he smiled.

"Does that mean you'll accept? Usually women are quite receptive to Jeff, but I know circumstances are different." His smile was contagious as he came closer to shake her hand. "You won't regret it."

"I think I'll regret it constantly, but I'll remind myself of what I'm getting. One year only."

"I intend to hire someone to take Jeff's place, so it might not be one year exactly, but close. You get your first payment and your new title and position today. I want you to start now. Jeff will be in soon to get on the payroll. Take this week to wind up what you are working on as much as you can. I'll have someone moved over to be my assistant. Your suggestions are welcome. I've already told Jeff he can handle the Cabrera line."

"You trust him to do well," she said, thinking about the premier line of boots and saddles they would start marketing. "Three generations of Brands have fought for that line. Now that you've got it, you're turning it over to your inexperienced brother," she said, thinking Noah might be losing his touch.

"Stop looking at me as if I've sprouted two heads," Noah said with amusement and she once again was reminded of his keen perception.

"Very well," she replied, feeling her face flush. "What time does your brother arrive?"

"Soon, I imagine. The front desk will just send him up. Holly, thanks for taking this offer. If you'll give Jeff half a chance, I don't think you'll be sorry."

"I'll try," she said stiffly, knowing she was going to have to remind herself daily of the financial reward. "I brought things to go over with you, but we'll do it later. My mind is spinning. My whole life changed!"

"Later works for me," he said easily. Scooping up her papers, she fled his office for the safety of her desk. She clung to the prospect of the money and advance in her career for taking this job.

She just hoped she wouldn't have cause to quit. She'd definitely have to return the first half of the payment. She thought of the picture of Noah with his brother—a cocky grin on his twin's face and a big Western hat tilted back on his head. In boots, he was taller than Noah in the picture and he'd worn hip-hugging jeans. She shivered and hoped she could last.

When Jeff passed through the front doors of the Brand Enterprises headquarters, revulsion rippled in him. Memories of working here in his twenties and how trapped he'd felt returned. His dad had been a continual overbearing presence, trying to micromanage the least decision.

Jeff's boot heels clicked on the polished marble floor of the entrance. He stopped at Security to tell the guard his name. He was given a badge to wear and ushered past the small office. He thought about the payment that would go into the bank today and his spirits lifted a fraction. One year and then he could do as he pleased again. He thought about the line of cutting horses he would like to raise. Surely, for one year, he could assume the uneasy weight of his father's legacy again.

The lobby was elegant and expensive—glass, marble, leather and greenery. An atrium flooded the center of the lobby with light. He was certain every item had been selected to impress all who entered—employees, competitors and customers. Noah could have decorated the lobby, but Jeff knew it had been the decorators his grandfather and his dad had hired, not his brother. Before their grandfather, Brand Enterprises headquarters had been without fancy trappings. He took the elevator to the top floor to see his brother.

As he walked down a hall and rounded a corner, a woman rushing in the opposite direction ran into him, spilling the papers she carried. Jeff reached out to steady her. "Sorry," he apologized.

"I'm sorry," she said. "I was lost in thought. I should have—" Huge green eyes riveted him and he drew a deep breath. Her perfume was as enticing as everything else about her. Her auburn hair was caught up in a clip behind her head. A few wayward tendrils escaped, the silky strands relieving the aloof perfection of her navy suit and silk blouse.

Consumed in the depths of her wide eyes, Jeff realized he was staring. He wondered how long she would gaze intently at him. As if she realized what she was doing, she blinked and wriggled away. Flawless skin, a straight nose and full red lips made him think of long, slow kisses. Her face was beautiful. She blinked as if coming out of a daze and glanced up at his hat. He could see the disapproval in her expression. Tight-lipped, she looked down. Toes of his alligator hand-tooled boots stuck out beneath the pant legs of his charcoal business suit. He detected her distaste and wondered who she was.

She knelt to gather her spilled papers and he leaned over to scoop them up. "I'll get them," he said, picking up papers quickly to hand them to her. His hand brushed her warm fingers.

"You're Jeff Brand, aren't you?" she said as if discovering a pit viper at her feet.

"Yes, I am," he replied, intrigued at her reaction. "You know me, but I don't believe I've had the pleasure—I wouldn't forget you," he said, offering his hand.

She shook her papers as if to indicate she couldn't shake hands for the papers she held, which was not true. "I'm Holly Lombard," she said with reluctance and then he guessed the cause of her frosty manner must be her new assignment with him.

"I suppose Noah has told you about me. I'm glad to meet you, Holly," Jeff said, dropping his hand and studying her, wondering if she had refused to work with him.

Judging from the cold reception, it seemed something more disastrous had happened. But he felt, with his entire being, that he was the cause of her icy animosity.

"We'll see each other later," she said and rushed past him.

"Yes, ma'am," he drawled, turning to watch her attractive figure disappear in a warren of cubicles. What a waste. She was stunning, but he was chilled from the encounter. How did Noah work with someone like Holly Lombard? He knew the answer as swiftly as the question had risen. Noah would be delighted with someone who was all business.

Shaking his head, Jeff proceeded on his way.

He was shown into his brother's office on the top floor. In amusement he glanced around at the handcrafted fruitwood desk, the dark wood paneling, the elegant oils on the walls. "I think you've topped Dad in the lavish office competition. This ought to intimidate the opposition. If they ever get in this rarefied atmosphere."

Noah laughed. "It's comfortable. You can have one here just like it if you want. I was afraid you might get cold feet and not show."

"You know me well. I kept thinking about the money going into my account today."

"I've already sent it to your bank and talked to your banker about it. It's done."

"Thanks. I just ran into Holly Lombard. If looks could kill, I'd be back there on the floor."

"Holly?" Noah sounded surprised momentarily until a sheepish grin spread on his face. "She's a little leery of working with you. You'll inspire her confidence quickly I'm sure. She worries you might be a bit inexperienced."

"She may be smarter than you. I am definitely rusty."

"Not really," Noah said dryly as he picked up folders and crossed the room to hand them to Jeff. "I want you to see these—the latest about the company. I know you already get them in the mail, but I also would guess that you don't read them."

"I read a few," Jeff said.

"Back to Holly. You might as well know—she's sour on men because her fiancé kicked her out and broke the engagement. She lives for her job and she's not enthused about working at your place. So your legendary charm's not going to work on her."

"I didn't used to question your business judgment, but she may not be the person for this job. Is she going to be uncooperative?"

"Holly? She's way too professional. If she has a job, she'll give it her best. You'll see. I just wanted to clarify why she may seem prickly." Noah spoke on his intercom and in minutes there was a light knock at the door.

"Come in. Holly, I think you've already met my brother, Jeff Brand. Jeff, this is your new assistant."

Jeff's pulse sped up as he watched the auburn-haired beauty he had collided with earlier. He walked toward her and offered his hand again, certain she would feel compelled to shake hands in Noah's presence.

She extended her hand, a gesture nullified by her glacial look. Yet the moment there was physical contact, he felt a tingle. As he gazed into her green eyes, he saw a glimmer of shock and realized she had felt sparks, too. She inhaled and then yanked her hand away, but the chemistry was there—she had been as aware of it as he was.

In that moment, the prospect of his new job made a subtle shift from dull to dangerous. He didn't want to experience any kind of fiery attraction to someone from the city who didn't like country living.

"I hope we can work together," he said and sincerely

meant it. She wasn't quite the snow queen he'd first imagined.

She gave him a frosty smile. "I've heard great things about you," she said.

"I'll see if I can live up to them," he said, wondering what Noah had done to get her agree to work for him, because he suspected it was a dilly.

"This morning I'll take Jeff to Human Resources to get his paperwork. This afternoon I've cleared my calendar at three. Can you do the same, Holly?"

"Of course," she answered smoothly.

"If you'll meet with us, I'll go over what I want Jeff to handle and we can get started. I've asked him to work in the office this week to get reacquainted with people, departments and sections. You'll start at his ranch next Tuesday."

Jeff noticed the color in her cheeks—she must view this whole endeavor as a fate worse than death. He wondered again if she would even cooperate with him. He guessed she would or Noah wouldn't have placed her in this position. Jeff sighed. Waste of a beautiful woman.

In minutes she was gone and he gave his brother a lopsided grin. "I can shake off the icicles now. You're sure she'll work with me at home?"

Noah smiled. "Holly's smart and I'm paying her plenty to do this. This is going to be great, Jeff. Thanks."

"Keep that thought in mind the first time we disagree."

Noah laughed. "I know we'll disagree, but we'll work it out."

TWO

Tuesday morning, the day of the dreaded move, Holly left her house in the dark. After driving from her North Dallas home and through Fort Worth, by fifteen minutes beyond Fort Worth, she realized she had glanced at the clock easily fifteen times. "I already hate this drive. Noah Brand, I'm beginning to dislike even you," she said in the quiet car.

It was a long, dull, uneventful drive away from city lights and civilization.

Last week Jeff Brand hadn't inspired any great trust. He'd listened and cooperated, offering little, his long legs stretched out and a lazy half-lidded look on his face as if he were daydreaming while she or Noah talked. Clearly, the easygoing cowboy had no ambition or he would have stayed with the company in the first place. She couldn't imagine being a cowboy as the epitome of success by anyone's measure. She gritted her teeth and envisioned a log house with chickens running in the yard and a wire fence surrounding the place to keep out cows. In spite of the warmth of her car she shivered.

"Noah, I hate you for this," she repeated, wondering how many more times she would say it in the coming year. Or if she'd quit.

She thought about the promotion and money and clamped her mouth closed. She would see this year through, no matter how remote this ranch was. She could do this. Where the light spilled onto the shoulders of the highway, she looked at miles of mesquite and cactus and barbed-wire fences. How could anyone choose to live out here in preference to a city? She had been born in a city and grown up in one. She knew nothing about country life.

Four hours each day, Tuesday through Friday, she would drive back and forth between here and Dallas. Her once good opinion of Noah Brand lowered another notch.

When she drove over a cattle guard and between two tall stone posts, daylight showed on the flat eastern horizon. Large iron gates opened when she pressed the electronic control Jeff had given her. A brown roadrunner dashed across the path of her car and she glared at the big bird. Ridiculous bird in an end-of-the-world place.

It was a surprisingly long drive before a privacy fence and more iron gates. To her amazement, her surroundings were transformed. Sprinklers turned on lush lawns and ponds held silvery fountains while live oaks were abundant. Still-dewy grass and leaves reflected the sunlight back at her. In a short time the ranch compound appeared and she realized she had underestimated Jeff Brand. She gazed at enough structures for a small town.

The ranch house was a sprawling two-story mansion that easily matched Noah Brand's palatial mansion. By any standards the ranch compound was impressive. She was taken aback, looking at the landscaped gardens surrounding the buildings. His easy manner had lulled her into envisioning him living in something barely inhabitable.

Sunlight splashed over roofs and gave a rosy glow to a myriad of colorful flowers. She fished out a piece of paper with directions, which she followed, stopping in front of what looked like a long, wood-and-stone ranch house. Gathering her purse, briefcase and laptop, she climbed out of the car.

Her reassessment continued as she crossed a wide wrap-around, air-conditioned porch enclosed in glass. The front door opened before she could ring the bell and her pulse jumped when she looked up into lively gray eyes and a smile that made her knees week. A shiver ran up her spine and in that instant, just as with their previous encounter, she forgot her animosity. Annoyance was consumed in a hot attraction that she felt to her toes.

"Morning," Jeff Brand said with a smile. His cotton Western shirt, jeans and boots were just another reminder of all the things wrong with this new assignment she'd been given. "Well, well, don't you look as pretty as a sunny morning." Jeff's warm voice didn't hold a degree of a brisk business attitude. "My day just brightened. You are going to make this job palatable."

"Thank you," she replied, gazing up at him and unable to break the spell that held her immobile.

Something flickered in his gaze and his smile widened a fraction. "How was your drive?" he asked, but she felt as if something else was happening between them and the conversation was incidental.

"Quiet, peaceful with no traffic," she answered, astounded by the pleasant words coming out of her mouth.

"Come in. Want some coffee before we begin?" Stepping back, he held the door, and when she looked away the spell was broken. Heat flooded her face as embarrassment poured over her. She had been as dazed as a young teen the first time a boy paid her any attention. Where was her brain? And telling Jeff the ride was peaceful—what was the matter with her? It had been a miserable drive—too long, too boring, too lonely. Wondering what kind of spell he wove, she entered the hallway.

"I see you brought the office with you," he said, glancing at her briefcase and laptop.

"Just some things I thought we should go over."

"First, let's go have a cup of coffee and we can talk about the day ahead. There's breakfast if you'd like."

"Mr. Brand—"

"It's Jeff. No 'Mr. Brand' please. I feel as if my dad ought to step out from somewhere nearby."

She drew herself up, trying to establish rules from the beginning. "I think we should keep everything strictly business as if we were at headquarters. We'll get more done that way," she said, knowing she sounded like a harpy, but unable to stop herself.

He smiled at her and his eyes twinkled as if he found every word she had said amusing, irritating her further. "Sure thing, Holly. Where did you ever get the name Holly? You don't hear it that often."

"My birthday is in December and my mother was carried away with having a Christmas baby. I'll need time this morning to move my things in," she continued briskly, trying to get right back to business.

"Don't bother with any of that. I'll get a couple of hands and we'll move your belongings. Relocating you is easy."

"I suppose that'll be the most efficient," she said. "Where is my office?"

"Right next to mine. You can decorate it to suit yourself. In the meantime, Noah sent some of your furniture from Dallas, so you have basics."

"I don't need anything fancy. We won't have clients coming to the office out here."

Grinning, he looked down at her. "You came into this kicking and screaming about as much as I did, didn't you? My brother is an arm-twister deluxe, but then so's our dad."

"I suspect I was kicking and screaming, as you put it, a lot more than you," she remarked stiffly. How could he joke about it? She couldn't find anything in the situation to be lighthearted about. Adding to her annoyance was the constant prickly awareness of Jeff Brand as a desirable man.

"I see you're ready for a day on the ranch," she remarked. He took the box from her, his fingers brushing hers in a slight touch that made her warm from head to toe.

"No need for formal dress out here. Matter of fact, you can come as casually as you please. It'll be the two of us plus two secretaries who will arrive tomorrow. No need for formality."

"I feel far more professional when I dress for work," she said with her frostiest tone. Really, how had they gotten on to the subject of clothing.

"Don't be too hard on the two secretaries we'll have if they choose to relax a little."

"If they get their work done efficiently, I can cut them some slack."

"That's good to hear. This is my office," he said, waving his hand at an open door, and she glanced inside a light, airy room with sliding glass doors that opened onto a patio. The whole scene seemed to be right out of a decorator's catalog with exotic blooming plants, greenery and brightly cushioned elegant furniture.

"Not exactly roughing it out here on the ranch, are you?" she said, moving on to her office. This sunny room held a large desk from headquarters, her fruitwood file cabinets and a conference table. A bathroom adjoined her office.

"I won't lack for space," she said. "I'll get started."

"Go right ahead."

He was all the things she didn't like rolled into one package. Her total opposite. She watched him walk out of the room, his boot heels scraping on the polished plank floor. How was she going to survive this year?

All morning she worked as if demons were after her—trying to lose herself in business, getting moved in and organized, looking over ad campaigns and letters from clients, making calls. As she replaced the receiver from a call, she looked up to see Jeff lounging in the doorway, leaning against the jamb—a pose she had never seen his brother do in their whole time working together. Noah was dynamic, businesslike, professional, ambitious and smart—at least up until this last fiasco he had placed her in.

"You can stay for dinner if you'd like. I'll eat at the house, unless you want me to bring dinner here to the office."

"Thank you, no. I'm going home and it's a long drive," she replied, glancing at her watch. "My word, I didn't realize it was so late." It was half-past seven, longer than she had intended to stay. "I'm accustomed to working until seven in the evening in Dallas. I can't do that here and then drive home."

"No, you can't. If that drive gets old…"

Her hopes soared that he was going to offer to work in Dallas and she smiled at him in anticipation.

"You might think about moving into my ranch house during the week. I have lots of room. We don't even have to see each other. It would save you the drive, the time, the gas, the wear on your car."

"Thanks, but I'll go home to Dallas," she said, thinking she wouldn't spend one night in the boonies. It was bad enough to spend her days here.

"Suit yourself," he said. "Tomorrow our secretaries will arrive. They told me they're getting a place in town to live. That's another option. I didn't make them the same offer I made you."

She knew why because she had seen them talking to him. In the Dallas office both had flirted as much as they dared and acted as if they had lost their wits around him. To give him credit, he had been polite, without flirting in return. She hoped to heaven she never behaved that way around Jeff Brand. It was bad enough already, but at least she had never once flirted with the man. Her chilly manner may have made him feel she could stay at his place without incident.

By the time she was home that night, she canceled the dinner she'd planned with her neighbor, Alexa Gray, because she was too tired to go anywhere. She ate, planned the next day, worked for about an hour, caught up on the few e-mails she had received and went to bed only to have disturbing dreams of a long, lean cowboy.

Both secretaries moved to a nearby small town and Holly envied them the forty-five-minute drive to work, but she couldn't stand living with little more than a few houses, a post office, a general store and a gas station with two mulberry trees in the entire windblown place.

Throughout the week she tried to maintain the same cool professional relationship on his ranch that she'd had at headquarters, but soon realized she was the only one of the four of them who was doing so. Jeff's natural, easygoing manner seemed infectious.

If Jeff Brand noticed or cared about her aloof manner, he gave no indication. Every morning he offered her breakfast and each morning she turned it down even though the smells were tempting and the one brief glimpse she'd had of the spread in the kitchen was mouthwatering. She knew both secretaries ate breakfast when they arrived, but Jeff always went to his office leaving them alone.

There were isolated moments when that intense awareness of him flared and burned brightly. If they got too close to each other, bending over a paper or reaching for the same report and brushed hands, the air all but crackled between them. Any physical contact, however slight, was scalding and she could see awareness in his expression, too.

Thursday afternoon of her second week on the ranch she worked late on clients' letters with Jeff. He finally pushed back and looked at her. "Quitting time. Why don't you let me take you out to dinner tonight and just stay at my house? We'll go eat at a great rib place. We can unwind and relax and you won't have that damn drive. Best ribs west of Fort Worth. Besides, they're predicting rain in Dallas."

She hated the drive more each day and he'd been businesslike all week, except for the occasional gleam in his eyes, but that was all. She was torn between wanting to skip the drive and accept his invitation or turn him down and avoid all socializing.

"If you've got to think it over this long, you might as well stay," he said, a smile lifting one corner of his mouth in an appealing look that made her forget work and the drive.

He was a disturbing presence; she suspected an evening with him would be anything but relaxing. "You've got yourself a deal, but I can't promise I'll be good company," she said.

"You don't have to be," he said, flashing her a warm smile. "Let's go up to the house. I need to wash up before dinner. The secretaries left two hours ago, so I'll just lock up here."

"Why do you even bother to secure the office? Everyone here works for you and you have fences and dogs and men around."

He shrugged. "Just one more deterrent if anyone decided to snoop around. This is safer. I'd think you'd feel better about it."

"I do. Just a little out of character for you to be cautious, isn't it?"

He grinned. "What an opinion you have of me," he said and she felt her cheeks burn with embarrassment. "Close up your office. Meet me at the front," he said and was gone.

She shut down her computer, wondering whether

she would regret this night, but the thought of the drive back to Dallas grew more odious with each passing day. She hurried to the front to find him waiting. He stood watching her walk toward him. Beneath his gaze her insides fluttered, causing her to wish she had simply gone home. Turning on an alarm, he locked the door.

"Want to walk? It isn't far and it's hot outside. Your car is safe here if you prefer walking."

"Sure. I've been sitting behind a desk all day. So have you, for that matter."

"For once we agree on something. Will wonders never cease?" he teased and she smiled.

"I didn't know we were that much in disagreement," she said. "It feels good to walk. It's a beautiful evening," she added, trying to get back on impersonal footing.

"That it does. You keep up amazingly well."

"Long legs," she said before she thought about her answer. As they started down the winding dirt drive, a snake slithered away into the grass. Horrified, she gasped and grabbed his arm.

"Jeff!"

"It's gone. Besides, I'm unarmed. I don't have any way to kill it right now. It's a rattler and we have a lot of them. Don't worry about it. That's about as close as one will ever get."

Revulsion swamped her. As far as she was concerned, this miserable place wasn't fit for human occupation. It was a good thing Noah Brand was nowhere in the vicinity, or he would hear another tirade from her.

"Why do you like it here?" she blurted and Jeff smiled.

"I love the quiet, the open spaces, the friendly people, the life of a cowboy. I like my horses and riding. By the way, do you like to ride?"

"Not at all," she replied quickly. "I was thrown from a horse when I was nine years old. I haven't been on one since."

Even though they went at a brisk pace, it was a long walk to his mansion and she couldn't keep from constantly checking the road and surroundings for snakes.

"Next week bring a swimsuit to keep here and if you stay over we can swim before dinner. A quick swim works out the kinks."

She couldn't imagine getting into a pool with him, much less a pool with snakes living in the surrounding area.

"Sure," she said, certain she would never do any such thing. She had intended to keep everything on an impersonal level. This dinner idea wasn't a good one, but she had gotten herself into it tonight. One time shouldn't be the end of the world. She'd had plenty of dinners with Noah and they were always filled with business.

When she crossed the wide patio to the main house, she realized the house was even larger than it had looked from the office. "This must go on for miles," she said as he held open the door, followed her in and turned off his alarm system.

As she walked through a wide hallway, she passed a spacious kitchen with an adjoining eating area and a fruitwood table that would seat sixteen easily.

"Don't you get lonely in this mansion all by yourself?"

He shook his head. "Nope. Until this job, I had lots of company staying here. During hunting season, I have friends here constantly. They come and go, but at present, I'm the only one home. Most of the time I don't use all of the house. No one person could, but I've gotten used to it. My staff maintains it. You'll meet some of them in the morning—Marc LeBeouf, my cook, for one."

She wondered how long she could live in such a place before she would take it for granted. "I have a room at the end of the hall," he said, turning to veer off into a hallway lined with open doors. Before they reached the door at the end, he pointed to a room a couple of doors away from his. "How's this?" he asked, stepping inside. She walked into an elegant bedroom suite with an adjoining sitting room.

"Amazing and lovely," she answered and he grinned.

"Did you think I lived in a log cabin?" Without waiting for an answer, he continued, "Give me twenty minutes and I'll meet you outside your door. Can I get anything for you?"

"No," she answered. "I'll be ready."

She closed her door and went to the spacious bath-room, pausing to look at the sunken tub, the potted plants, a beach mural on one wall and full-length mirrors on another wall. Each room she had seen had been luxurious, indicating a decorator's planning. Jeff Brand had surprising facets to his personality.

She took out her comb and unfastened her hair. She combed it, starting to let it fall free and then changed her mind. She still wanted a wall of reserve between them because the chemistry was volatile. She clipped her auburn hair at the back of her head, allowing a few tendrils to fall loosely around her face.

Smoothing her navy slacks and matching silk blouse, she wondered where they were going and if she would be the only one not wearing jeans. She didn't care. Just get through the evening.

When she left the bedroom, he was waiting in the hall as promised. Her pulse jumped at the sight of him in a fresh white shirt tucked into tight, hip-hugging jeans that spanned a narrow waist.

A wide-brimmed hat was pushed to the back of his head. He was all male, appealing, yet all the things she didn't like. Once again she wondered why she hadn't just said no and driven back to Dallas.

"Think ribs," he said with amusement. "You look as if you're going to a disaster."

"Sorry. It's been a long day."

"That it has. We'll see what we can do to put a smile on your face."

"Don't make me a project. Just to sit and relax and have a good dinner will be enough."

"Good deal," he said.

He'd showered and his hair was still damp, the slight wave more noticeable. His aftershave was enticing and his shirt was crisp. She suspected he would have plenty of women tonight who would be happy to see him.

In minutes, he held open the door to a sleek black sports car where she nestled into the soft leather seat.

It was half an hour to a large log structure with a red roof. Inside, musicians played while couples circled the floor doing the two-step. As he led her to a booth, people constantly stopped him to say hi. At the booth he sat facing her and in seconds a waitress who knew him handed them both menus.

They ordered platters of ribs and as soon as they were alone, Jeff stood and reached for her hand. "Let's dance."

She had a vague memory of doing a two-step at a college dance.

"I'm rusty," she said as she slid out of the booth. "If it's too bad, we sit down and some of those women who stopped you on the way in will dance with you, I'm sure."

"You'll get it, it's easy," he said. He turned her beside him as he took her hands to step with others circling the floor. In minutes she was enjoying herself. She remembered the simple step. It was a relief to do something physical after an exhausting week driving and sitting behind a desk for hours at a stretch.

Locks of her hair fell out of the clip, but she ignored them. Jeff was light on his feet—no surprise. In all the time she had known Noah, she had never danced with him, but dancing wasn't anything they would have done, either. Their relationship was strictly business.

"Our ribs are probably getting cold," Jeff said between dances. "Want to go eat?"

"Sure," she said. "Dancing was fun—a break from this week's routine." Just before she sat in their booth, he caught her arm and turned her to face him.

"We can improve on the evening," he said and she looked up at him with curiosity. Her pulse already raced from his hand on her arm, but it jumped again as he reached behind her head and unfastened the clip holding her hair, which spilled over her shoulders.

"Jeff!" she said, annoyed, yet aware of him standing close.

"That's a lot better. Let's eat," he said, taking off his hat and dropping the clip in it beside him on the seat.

In consternation she shook her head, feeling her long hair swirl across her shoulders. She didn't like him taking charge, didn't want her hair down with him.

Her hair falling loose made things just a degree more informal between them. It was bad enough that she was eating and dancing with him.

Trying to keep that invisible barrier between them, she ate in silence, feeling doomed if she didn't because he was a charmer. She had learned that much the first hour she met him.

"What do you need? I'll get our waitress."

She looked at the platter of steaming ribs with sauce spilling over them, golden corn bread, pale green coleslaw. She shook her head. "This is fine. I don't need anything."

"This is the best way to end the day," he said.

As she ate the tender, juicy meat, she realized he was correct in raving about how good the ribs would be. When she told him, he paused.

"Trust me on ribs. I'm a rib connoisseur."

"I'll remember," she said. "Great dancer, good judge of ribs."

"Ahh, thank you. An area where I have your approval."

"You have my approval," she said, embarrassed now.

He gave her a doubting look. "I don't think so."

"We're out of the office. This is different. I have ideas about how things should be done at the office. Don't you think you would get more accomplished if you worked at headquarters?"

"I don't know," he replied after a moment. "Maybe, maybe not, but I can't bear the thought of the corporate world. If Noah needs my help, I'm happy to give it, but we do it my way."

Her disapproval of him returned. So much more

could be accomplished if he stayed in Dallas. She loved the bustle of the office and the city.

They were quiet for a time and then he asked about her family.

"Dad's a banker in Houston, Mom is a dermatologist. I have two brothers. Chuck is an attorney in Washington and Pierce is a doctor in New York."

"Impressive family. That's where you get your drive," he said.

She shrugged. "I suppose. We just were expected to do well. Your family isn't very different. Look at your dad and your brother. Yourself for that matter. You excelled in your own field."

"I'll admit you're right. I guess you and I are more alike then you thought."

"In the force, perhaps," she said with disdain, thinking she wasn't one degree like Jeff Brand, nor would she ever be.

"Are those brothers of yours married?"

"Both married, no children," she said, sipping her water. "That was a delicious dinner."

"One place where we get along—out there on the dance floor. Ready again or want to just sit?"

"I'll dance. I told you, it feels good to move," she said, thinking a two-step was about the most neutral dance she could do with him. So far there had been no variation, no slow dancing, so she felt comfortable returning to the dance floor.

Since her breakup she had been off men. She was thankful he hadn't asked one question about her love life. Noah must have filled him in. Before tonight, she wouldn't have thought she'd go out with any man for any reason, but this had been impersonal and she suspected Jeff was no more thrilled to be with her than she was with him. Even as that thought went through her mind, there was a nagging reminder about their mutual attraction and she knew she needed to keep up her guard around him. Physically, Jeff Brand was a charming, sexy, appealing man.

It was just the rest of the package that she couldn't handle.

She stopped thinking about anything—just enjoying the dance and moving, not caring what he was thinking.

Finally, she tugged on his hand. "That's about all the fun I can stand for one night. I'd like to go back to the ranch." The words sounded hollow to her ears. She hoped there would be no awkward moments at his house.

As they returned to their booth, he held her arm lightly. They were quiet on the ride back to the ranch. Switching off the alarm at his house, he turned. "Want a drink? I have all sorts of stuff—pop, tea, coffee, milk, wine—whatever you'd like."

"Thanks, but I'm finished for today. I can get an early start tomorrow since I won't have the drive here."

Digging in his pocket, he held out her hair clip. "You might want this back. I like your hair the way it is now," he said and his voice had lowered a notch. He moved a step closer as he handed her the clip and she took it from him.

"Thanks." She looked up and was then ensnared in his gray eyes that had darkened with desire.

"Jeff," she said, meaning to end the evening and go, but his name came out breathlessly and she stood riveted. Her heart thudded and her temperature climbed. Her gaze drifted down to his mouth and then back to meet his eyes. It was impossible to breathe.

"Why not?" he whispered and leaned forward, covering her mouth with his.

Her heart slammed against her ribs. Heat flooded her. Desire kindled and the kiss sizzled as he stepped closer to slip his arm around her waist. His mouth pressed more firmly, his tongue sliding deep inside her mouth. She stopped kissing him and he leaned away a fraction.

"Jeff, we shouldn't," she protested, but her words were faint. All she could do was look at his mouth and want his kiss.

"Yes, we should," he whispered, pulling her close again and leaning down to kiss her. His kiss became passionate, urgent and demanding. She couldn't resist sliding one arm around his neck. She was reacting without thinking. Taking what she wanted, giving him what he demanded as she returned his kiss fully. There was no holding back, no hesitation.

She kissed him, desire consuming her while she ran her hand up the strong column of his neck and then combed her fingers through his thick hair. He leaned over her, his kiss going deep, a joining that would change their relationship forever.

Some dim voice stirred a faint protest deep within her. She ignored it, still clinging to him and kissing him back, need escalating with each second. Her pulse roared in her ears, shutting out all other sounds. She could feel his heart pounding against her own.

Finally, after forever, she realized how she was pouring herself into their kiss. Taking and giving fully. She came up out of fuzzy depths to reality, breaking the kiss and stepping back while her heart raced.

Jeff's breathing was as ragged as hers and he looked

stunned. She felt ambushed, caught up in something she never expected to happen.

"No," she whispered. "We're not going there. Not ever again," she said more clearly. She turned and hurried away, going up the stairs to the room he had given her, closing the door and touching her mouth as fury and horror mounted swiftly.

She didn't want his kiss. She was still trying to get over a breakup. Didn't want to be emotionally involved with any man right now, especially Jeff. She shouldn't have kissed him, danced with him or eaten with him. She raked the back of her hand across her mouth. Her lips still tingled. How could she have fallen into that trap?

She realized he had looked surprised and less than happy himself, but she didn't know him well enough to know what his feelings were. She didn't care. She was going to go home tomorrow after work. There were other jobs.

She stormed to the bathroom, scrubbed her face and yanked off her clothes to get into the shower as if she could wash away the evening and all her memories. Memories that already tormented her.

How would she ever sleep? How would she forget his kiss? Why had it been so spectacular?

She let warm water pour over her while her entire body sizzled. Physically she wanted him. That's what drove her fury. She had enjoyed his kiss, returned it passionately, more than enjoyed it. His kiss had been sensational.

She groaned and clenched her fists. She would go back to Dallas, go in Monday morning, resign and tell Noah he could have every penny back.

After getting dumped and kicked out of their place

by her ex-fiancé, she didn't want to get involved in any kind of relationship at this point in her life. She wasn't working with Jeff Brand. Noah could just forget it.

The prospect didn't make her feel one degree better. And it didn't help in forgetting Jeff's kiss. Why had she gotten herself into this job and this evening?

Three

Walking through the house, Jeff stopped in the kitchen to get a glass of milk. He thought about Holly, contemplating the kiss that had set him on fire. That ice was only a veneer. Her scalding blaze had broiled him to cinders.

He wanted her. Yet lust was a two-edged sword. He wanted her and he didn't want to desire her. She was the last female on earth he wanted to get involved with. He knew there was no danger. She felt the same way. From day one she'd made it clear he wasn't the type of man she associated with. What had her former fiancé been like?

The kiss had been an impulse and one he should have avoided. It had done no good for either one of them. He suspected she would be in a huff over it and chillier than ever.

Leave Miss Icicle alone. He wouldn't invite her out

for dinner or dancing. Her anger had been practically a tangible substance. But he didn't see how one harmless kiss could do that much damage.

Only, that kiss hadn't been harmless. He suspected he was going to have trouble sleeping tonight. Physically, he wanted more. Logically, he knew he needed to keep a distance between them. And not yield to impulse again.

"Dammit," he whispered, drinking his milk and rinsing his glass. He switched off the lights, went out to his cabana, changed quickly and jumped into his pool to swim laps, wearing himself down until he cooled.

He finally went to his room, seeing no light beneath her door. If she was asleep now, she would be up and gone in the morning when he got up. Yet he didn't think she'd walk back to the office in the dark. She was skittish about being in the country and the first critter she heard ought to ruin her nerves.

Stretching out in bed, he placed his hands behind his head. There had been a moment this evening when he'd spun her around and that thick auburn hair of hers had swung out and swirled across her cheek. The passionate woman beneath the ice had unfurled in a similar way, but he didn't care to explore the possibility.

It was nearly dawn before he fell into a restless sleep filled with erotic dreams about Holly.

Friday morning her door remained closed and he wondered several times if she was even in her room or if she had actually braved the wild animals in the dark.

In the kitchen he greeted his cook, and learned that Holly hadn't been seen yet. Leaving Holly to meet the other staff on her own, he went to the office.

About half-past eight she appeared with no apologies for being late. Despite that minor professional lapse, she was all business and that suited him fine. He didn't need a city-girl romance complicating his one-year office term.

All day she was coolly polite, ice once more. At five o'clock she told him goodbye. He stood at the front window and watched her drive away, regretting more than ever that he had kissed her.

It didn't take long on Monday for Noah to tear into him. "What the hell went on with you two last week?"

"Don't get in an uproar. We just went out to eat. What's the deal?"

"She was ready to quit. I can't get anything out of her about it, but she was happy when she left here last Monday."

"She didn't quit?"

"No. I talked her into staying," Noah said, frowning.

"Well, nothing went on, but you've known from the start that she doesn't like the ranch, me or the drive out to either."

Noah stared at him and Jeff stared back until Noah shook his head and picked up a folder. "Well, maybe it's the drive and being away from here. Maybe she feels out of touch."

"Probably so," Jeff said, not caring if she did quit except he knew she was bringing him on in the job much quicker than he could possibly do on his own. She was bright and knew the business just as Noah had said. "Dad called and asked me to dinner tonight. I can't imagine what brought on the invitation. Maybe it's a peace offering. I don't suppose you and the family are included by any chance?"

"Nope, just you and Dad," Noah said, picking up papers and motioning to a nearby table. "Let's move over there. I want you to see these." Noah shed his charcoal suit jacket and hung it on the back of a chair. Jeff had shed his jacket the minute he walked into his office and wished he could ditch his tie.

"How's the Cabrera line coming?" Noah asked. "Do you like our promotional campaign to introduce the boots?"

"Yes and I had the secretaries make an appointment for lunch with Emilio Cabrera and I'm taking Holly with me."

"Good move. He seems to like her. Now on to the Markley stores. That's a chain I've given to you to handle."

They continued talking and Jeff forgot Holly. He saw little of her throughout the day. Once he left his office and saw her farther down the hall talking to someone. Today she wore a conservative green suit with a calf-length skirt that hid her legs. As buttoned-up as ever, he thought, but he remembered her kiss that had been anything but cold.

He wondered how the coming week would go. If she had almost quit her job, their kiss must have gotten to her. The thought amused him.

By eight o'clock he sat in his father's study. Dinner had gone relatively pleasantly, but he suspected something was coming that he didn't want to hear. This chummy evening was so uncharacteristic of his father that he knew better than to think his dad had changed.

He tried to focus on what his dad was saying, knowing they were coming to the point of this evening. Watching his father, Jeff could see how he had aged this past year with deeper lines in his face and circles beneath his eyes.

Knox stood turning an unlit pipe in his hand. He'd had to give up smoking and Jeff knew Knox was having difficulty cutting the habit. All sympathy for him was squashed by his certainty that his dad was still going strong with his meddling habit.

"Jeff, I'm going to make you the offer that I did before. I want to see both of my sons married and settled. The million-dollar bonus I offered each of you if you married this year still stands. You have to remain married at least a year, although I hope longer."

Jeff clamped his jaw shut and drew a deep breath, trying to hold on to his patience. Before his father's heart surgery, Jeff would have walked out at this point in the conversation. Since the surgery, Jeff was watching the man who had once been strong and invincible to his sons become frail and all too mortal. Reminding himself that since adulthood, he and his father had rarely agreed about the direction his life should take, Jeff listened in silence.

"I'll keep that in mind, Dad. At the moment there's no prime candidate."

"That may be," Knox said, strength coming into his tone and bringing with it a flicker of the man his dad used to be. "I didn't figure you'd be overly interested because you weren't before, so I have another incentive that I think will interest you."

Fully attentive now, Jeff leaned in. This couldn't be good.

"If you'll marry within the next six months, in addition to the money, I'll give you the family ranch at that time. I'll make it up to Noah with money or a bigger share of Brand Enterprises—Noah won't want the ranch, anyway."

Shocked, Jeff stared at his father, no longer hearing what Knox was saying. The family ranch. "And if I don't marry in the next six months?" Jeff asked, realizing his dad was determined to get his way.

"I'll sell that ranch to Paul Watterman, who wants it and will pay me high dollar for it. Your mother doesn't care, nor does Noah."

"Dammit, Dad," Jeff let slip, clenching his fists. "The ranch has been in our family for generations. Why let this ruin that?"

"I regret using such leverage, but I'd like to see you settled soon. I've told you my reasons."

"I'll think about it," Jeff said, knowing he needed to get away from his dad before he said something he'd regret or something that would give his dad a rise in blood pressure or worse. He stood. "I better get going. It's a long drive to the ranch. I enjoyed dinner with you and I'll consider your offer. You take it easy."

"I enjoyed dinner, too, Jeff. Now that you're in town regularly, I hope we see more of you. Next time, I'll see to it that Mother can be with us. She was disappointed to miss you, but this trip to shop in Houston with her friends has been planned for months."

"Next time I'll take you and Mom out."

Knox was still a bit too weak to see him out, so Jeff hurried to his car. A need to do something physical to let off steam built with every step. The family ranch was the prize his dad was dangling, one that his dad knew he wanted.

Jeff struck the steering wheel as he drove, mulling over the proposition, tempted to grab some woman who was fun to be with, propose and get the ranch with a temporary marriage.

He swore aloud in the car as he drove, giving vent to all the things he wished he could say to his dad.

He was on his own property when his cell phone rang and he answered to hear his uncle's voice.

"Jeff, are you home?" Shelby said.

"Almost."

"How was your week?"

"Bearable," Jeff said. "Monday I go in and then the rest of the week, I'm at the ranch."

"I still think you're crazy for accepting."

"I hope I can make it through the year," Jeff said lightly, relaxing because he enjoyed his uncle whether they agreed on the topic of conversation or not.

"I know what Knox offered you tonight. He ran it past me, probably to annoy me. My meddling brother is always interfering. I wondered if this time you're giving some thought to what he wants."

"Nope. As badly as I want that ranch, I haven't changed any more than Dad. He isn't going to run my life."

Shelby chuckled. "Not surprised. Jeff, you can buy yourself a second ranch bigger than the family one. Just let it go and don't look back. No wonder my brother had a heart attack. He's so wound up about every detail of his life and Noah's and yours. Now he'll have Noah's baby to meddle with."

"I won't argue any of that," Jeff said. His dad and his uncle had fought all their lives. "Thank goodness Noah and I get along a degree better than you and Dad."

"I'm glad you do. My overbearing older brother gets my goat and always has."

"I know."

"Don't let him get yours. Work a month and then take a week's vacation and meet me in Monte Carlo. We'll party every night and you'll lose the business pressures."

"Thanks, Uncle Shel," Jeff said, smiling. "I'll keep that offer in mind. In the meantime, if you come to Texas, we can get together when I'm in Dallas."

"Better go now. We'll talk again soon—I should be in Texas sometime soon. In the meantime, keep your cool and outfox my brother."

Jeff laughed again. "Thanks for the call." Jeff broke the connection, feeling a closeness and warmth toward his uncle that he had rarely ever felt for his dad. While he knew part of it was Shelby's personality, part of it was Shelby's own friction with his older brother. Another part was that Shelby had always been on Jeff's side in family disputes while Knox had been on Noah's. Jeff reflected how thankful he had been for his uncle when he was a child.

As soon as Jeff climbed out of his car at home, he hurried to the barn where he kept some old clothes. He changed swiftly, switched floodlights on the closest corral, found one of the wildest horses they had and in minutes was atop riding a bucking bronco thoughts of Brand Enterprises and his father's offer gone.

A week later on a July Sunday night Holly had dinner with her neighbor from the adjoining condo. Tall and slender with a mop of brown curls, Alexa was successful in real estate. Holly felt a bond with her because they were both wrapped up in their work. As they ate in a quiet restaurant while a string quartet played softly in the background, she listened to Alexa talk about her company's latest listing.

Smiling at her friend, Holly sipped a cup of hot green tea. "Your career is rising and I feel as if mine is mired in quicksand."

"Don't be ridiculous. Just keep doing what you're doing—look at what you're getting out of this deal," Alexa said briskly.

Holly glanced at her watch. "I have that dreadful drive in the morning, so we better call it a night."

"If it's so terrible, move into his ranch house during the week. I've been saying that forever. You said it's a palatial mansion. You wouldn't have to see him."

Holly gathered her purse and thought about the Thursday night she stayed at Jeff's. "I don't know. It's tempting when I see those secretaries breeze in after their short drive. If he'd move out, I might do it."

They both smiled and the subject was dropped as they drove home.

"Keep thinking about the money," Alexa said as they parted at the walkway between their condos.

The drive bothered Holly more each day, yet the thought of living in the same house with Jeff was equally undesirable. And the quiet at the ranch…she felt as if they were the only people on the earth. She had never thought much about the noise in the city. Her condo seemed quiet enough, but she knew now there was nowhere in Dallas she had ever been as still as that ranch. Only the sound of wind or a bird broke the silence much of the time and it added to the isolated, solitary feeling that enveloped her when she was there. She shivered and stepped out on her patio just to listen to sounds of the city—in the distance a faint rumble of traffic, a dog barking, small noises she took for granted. She couldn't imagine why Jeff loved the place so much, but then she didn't understand much about him anyway.

On Tuesday morning, Holly thought again about her conversation with Alexa. Even though summer had the best possible weather and the longest days, she still had to drive in the dark. She often did in Dallas, but short drives were different.

When she passed through the entrance gates she heard a bang and in seconds realized she had a flat tire. Frustration made her want to scream, but she kept calm and called Jeff to tell him she would be late. He said he would be right there.

She hated to get out of the car, wondering what varmints were in the high grass. Taking a deep breath with her flashlight in hand, she stepped out and swung the light all around her, praying she didn't see anything looking back at her.

Wind was a soft whisper and the horizon was graying to the east. Shortly the sun would appear. She looked at the darkness surrounding her and the sky overhead that held what looked like millions of stars, realizing she had never seen a sky like this before.

Positive she could hear little critters in the grass around her, she hurried to open the trunk and set out the tools. She suspected she could never get the lug nuts off since they were put on with a machine. She kicked the flat tire lightly in disgust.

In a short time she heard a motor as headlights cut the darkness. Jeff parked and climbed out of a black pickup, leaving on his lights. In jeans, a short-sleeve sport shirt and boots, he still made her pulse jump at the sight of him and now, out here on this empty ranch road, he was an even more welcome sight.

Her reaction to him was a phenomenon she would never understand, but one that occurred consistently. Along with it came an awareness about herself and a ridiculous tendency to want to smooth her hair. She noticed wind whipping her slacks and knew she would never wear a skirt to the ranch.

Why, why, why had she let her guard down and returned his kiss? She shook her head.

"Hey, you already started to change the tire. You didn't need to do that," he said, his voice bringing her back to the situation at hand.

"I can't get the lug nuts loose."

"You ever changed a tire?" he asked, checking the jack and then hunkering down to turn the wrench.

"Yes, my brothers made sure of it. This is a new car with new tires, so a flat is frustrating."

He squinted up at her. "It happens. May just be a faulty tire. Still say you should move in and save yourself so much hassle," he said as he worked. Locks of his black hair fell over his forehead and she still puzzled over her reaction to him when there was no such thing with his twin brother. They looked identical, only she had no difficulty knowing which one she was with. In addition, she had noticed that Jeff had a tiny scar along his jaw. Probably from some daredevil stunt. She didn't want to ask.

Dropping nuts and bolts into the hubcap with loud clinks, he removed the tire and stood, turning to face her. "Want to?"

"What?"

"Move in. Try it this week and if you don't like staying on the ranch, move out."

She gazed into the darkness beyond him. "You don't think we would bother each other?"

"Nope. We didn't last time. Main house will be more convenient than a guesthouse," he said as he carried the flat toward his pickup. "Move in and give it a try."

"I suppose it's worth trying," she said.

"Good. I can get the guys to check out your tire."

"Don't bother. It's under warranty. I'll get a new one," she said and watched as he carried it easily to place it in her trunk.

"Thanks."

"It was nothing. I'm glad you were on the ranch when it happened and off the highway." He stood wiping his hands on a rag, but he was close in front of her and he paused to look at her. Again, that electrical current sparked between them. Held by his gaze, she remembered his kiss totally, feeling as drawn to him as she had that moment when he had leaned down to kiss her.

With an effort she turned away to get into her car, flustered, breathless and annoyed. "I'll see you at the office." She flung the words at him without looking back. She glanced in the rearview mirror to see him make a sweeping turn and follow her.

And she had agreed to move into his mansion.

She was relieved to be caught up in work that didn't involve him most of the day—they saw little of each other.

Alexa arrived at the condo that night the same time as Holly.

"I was going to call you tonight," Holly said. "I'm moving to his ranch for the rest of the week. If it works out, I'll stay there during the week most of the time."

"Good! That will be easier for you. You'll like the job better, I'll bet."

"I'll see how it goes. Cowboy Jeff said we can stay out of each other's way."

"If it's as palatial as you described, that shouldn't be a problem," Alexa said.

"Noah's urging me to stay out there, too. If Jeff were Noah, I wouldn't have to give it a moment's thought."

"You're working there anyway. I'll keep an eye on things around here. Want any plants watered?"

"No, thanks. I won't be away that long."

"True, the week will be over before you know it," Alexa said, running her fingers through her curly cap of brown hair.

"I hope," Holly replied. "I'll see you this weekend." She returned to her condo to pack, spending another restless night dreaming about Jeff Brand.

Wednesday at the office she hardly saw Jeff, and his absence allowed her to throw herself into her work until she heard a knock at the door and looked up to see him lounging there.

"I'm calling it a night. The secretaries left two hours ago."

"Good heavens, what time is it?" she asked, glancing at the clock. Surprised, she saw it was twenty after seven. "I think I've been sitting for the past hour," she said, standing and gathering up papers. "I'll have to drive to your house because I brought some things to keep there. You can ride with me."

"Sure. Close up and we'll go," he said and disappeared down the hall. She heard his boot heels on the bare floor as he walked away.

The minute she stepped through the door in his path a blast of hot air struck her. Even though her car was parked beneath a cover, heat enveloped her when she opened the door. As she switched on the motor and air-conditioning, he climbed into the car beside her, moving folders to the back. "Taking work home?" he asked.

"A little," she admitted, knowing he probably disapproved and would never do the same himself.

"You and Noah—work, work, work. Did you bring a swimsuit?"

"No, I forgot all about that," she said.

"Well, I'll swim later, but you might as well have dinner with me. I can grill a couple of steaks in no time."

"You don't..."

"I know I don't need to," he interrupted with amusement. "You have to eat and we're doing fair to middlin' together."

"Sure," she said, yielding because she suspected he wasn't giving up easily and she was hungry now that she thought about it.

Picking up her bag, he led her upstairs. "I can put you in a different wing or back to the same room you had before. You won't interfere with me there." He turned to look down at her as they reached the top of the stairs. "And I promise I won't interfere with you."

She couldn't keep from smiling in return. "Fine," she said, wondering where all her intentions had gone to get far away from him.

He set her things in the same bedroom. "I'll see you downstairs shortly. I can fix a drink—what would you like?"

"Iced tea would be great. Give me about fifteen minutes."

"No hurry," he said and was gone, but his presence permeated the room. She still wondered if she was making a huge mistake by staying here.

SARA ORWIG 57

Wearing her same slacks and blouse, she joined him on the patio. He had his back to her and he had changed to a knit shirt and slacks. Steaks smelled delicious as smoke spiraled in the air from the grill.

Water splashed from fountains in the pool and pots of exotic flowers added a festive air. The place should have been relaxing, but her nerves were raw in Jeff's disturbing presence.

Jeff turned and his gaze swept over her. Beautiful package that covered pure ice. Not so, he contradicted his own thoughts. There was fire somewhere beneath that ice. Red-hot and enticing. What a waste. He picked up a frosty glass of amber liquid and held it out.

"Your tea, Holly," he said, her name rolling off his tongue. He saw the flicker in her eyes and the quick intake of her breath. They had some kind of chemistry between them and he suspected she loathed that she couldn't control it. She was all about control. At least up to a point and then that attraction they both felt overwhelmed and consumed them, wreaking all kinds of havoc.

He turned away to tend the steaks and thought about his dad's offer. Jeff turned around again to study Holly as she looked over his patio. He realized she might be the way to get even with his father and get the family ranch at the same time. A marriage of convenience with Holly.

The instant the thought came, he rejected it. She hated men right now—was not into relationships. He couldn't imagine life with his total opposite. As he turned the steaks, arguments assailed him. Her low opinion of men could work in his favor. She wouldn't want any marriage to last. But a marriage of convenience would be a business contract and wouldn't be a real relationship in any manner. Jeff stared at the smoldering grill and listened to the steaks sizzle and pop. Set up a marriage of convenience with Holly and get the ranch and then dissolve the whole thing. Could he ever talk her into going for it?

He felt sure he could because Noah had talked her into this year-long situation. This would simply be an added layer.

Noah had all the faith in the world in her. Jeff didn't know her well, but he didn't see that it would matter. Holly would never want to stay married, cause him trouble or try to take advantage of his wealth.

The more he thought about it, the more feasible it seemed. He walked up to her. "Like what you see?" he asked.

"This is lovely. It's an oasis out here." She turned to face him and he met her level stare with his own. A faint breeze toyed with tendrils of her hair and he felt more confident by the second that they could pull off a marriage of convenience if he could talk her into it.

His gaze lowered to her mouth and she drew a deep breath. He wanted to kiss her again and at this moment, it was clear she wanted him to.

"Jeff," she whispered, stepping back slightly.

He slipped his hand behind her head into her soft, silky locks. "Shh, Holly. Just a kiss..." He leaned forward and when she started to turn away, he placed his mouth on hers.

Her lips were soft, warm, luscious. Her eyes closed and she placed her hand lightly on his shoulder.

His tongue slipped into her mouth and then hers into his as she returned his kiss. While they kissed, he took her drink and set it on a nearby table with his own.

He wrapped both arms around her, pulling her close

against him, her soft curves setting him on fire and reaffirming all he'd thought about her. Beneath the ice was a raging blaze. She was a fiery lover, but a woman who would have no emotional investment in a marriage. For his purposes, she might be the perfect bride.

Four

Jeff's kiss erased their differences leaving temptation in its wake. The thoughts of the ranch, working in a nowhere office—not one mattered when they kissed. They had a torrid, intense attraction that had nothing to do with the rest of their lives. Except she knew better. Dimly, she struggled to pull her wits together. This way lay disaster.

Finally she stopped him and he released her. As before, she was dazed. His gray eyes held desire so blatant that she wanted to walk right back into his embrace.

"Jeff, this is exactly what I was worried about. I don't want an affair on the side."

"Sure," he said, smiling at her as he inhaled deeply and turned away.

Nice speech, she told herself, watching him return to his cooking. She may have interrupted things for now, but she couldn't stop the raging desire that he had ignited. She walked away, trying to cool down and get herself together.

To her surprise, he must have decided to heed what she told him. Through dinner and into the evening, he was charming, but there was nothing physical, very little flirting. Time slipped away from her. She knew it had to be getting late. When she glanced at her watch, she saw it was one o'clock.

"I don't stay up until one on weeknights," she said.

"You'll survive and we can be late tomorrow."

"No. Let's keep on schedule. I'm turning in now. I've enjoyed dinner and the evening, but you don't have to cook for me every night," she said.

"Most of the time Marc is here and I have dinner cooked and ready. The change of pace is nice."

She had a prickly awareness of him, thinking about their kiss early in the evening. At her door she left him.

All evening after their kiss, he had done as she asked. He had been amiable, pleasant, but nothing more. It hadn't cooled her desire or awareness of him a whit.

If there were no more kisses, could she get so she viewed him with the same detachment she viewed other men? She didn't think she could if she lived here for the rest of the year.

Of all the strange places to find this sizzling chemistry...

During the rest of the week and into the next, Jeff was the same. Congenial, courteous and professional. Not that it helped her attraction to him. Far from it. She grew more aware of him, more tingly around him with each passing day, though they returned to their routine.

Thursday afternoon she was exhausted, warm even in the air-conditioned office and decided to stop for the day. She looked into Jeff's office and saw he was on the phone with his head bent over his desk as he wrote.

She quietly left him alone. The secretaries had quit about half an hour earlier.

As she drove to the house in her hot car, she thought about taking a swim. Jeff was still working. She could get a quick, solitary dip in the pool, plus get a little workout.

She pulled on her new swimsuit, a one-piece that she wouldn't have selected before this job. Her cover-up was longer than usual, a blue cotton that actually was a cover. Relieved to have the pool to herself, she dropped her things on a chair and jumped into the cool, inviting water.

She swam laps and then paused at the deep end.

"You ran off without me," Jeff said. She turned to see him approaching the pool.

The sight of him stirred butterflies in her stomach. "You were busy working and on the phone so I didn't want to disturb you. The drive home was so hot I thought I'd get a quick dip in your pool."

"Good idea," he said before he sliced into the water and swam the length of the pool. To her surprise, while they swam, he kept a distance between them. In spite of his impersonal behavior, she was more mindful than ever of his broad shoulders, muscled chest with a mat of dark hair, and his almost naked, muscled body.

"I'm getting out. You swim as long as you like."

"I'll go change, too," she said. "This has been refreshing."

How innocuous their conversation that did nothing to cool her fiery consciousness of both their bare bodies.

When she climbed out, her face flushed and she hoped he thought it was due to exertion if he even noticed. She slipped into the cover-up and hurried to her room to shower and change.

She had bought jeans for the occasion and wore a plain cotton blouse, trying to fit in to a degree. Boots—never.

Looking every inch a cowboy, he was ready and waiting in jeans, a Western shirt and boots and her pulse sped a notch the minute she saw him.

Throughout the evening he was his usual entertaining self and she was beginning to wonder about the change in him. Maybe he had just taken her at her word… Except there was that look in his eyes. That hadn't changed one bit. It was as hot and blatant as ever.

All evening, as before when they'd been in public, women came by to talk and flirt with him. She never expected him to spend so much of his time with her because there was nothing between them except the job and it was obvious plenty of women would have been happy for his attention.

When the music changed to a waltz, he drew her into his arms to dance with her, circling the floor, talking about the ranch and an upcoming rodeo. His aftershave was inviting. He was light on his feet, an excellent dancer, which didn't surprise her.

The music ended, followed by more fast two-steps. She finally turned to him. "Jeff, tomorrow is a working day. I should go."

"Sure."

On the drive to the ranch he kept her entertained and when they left the car, he draped his arm across her shoulders in an uncustomary gesture, yet his conversation was still warmhearted and impersonal.

"Let's have something to drink. I won't keep you up late, but I want to talk to you."

Curious, she nodded, wondering if he wanted her to move out or make some job changes. She couldn't imagine him talking to her about job changes now. She couldn't guess what was on his mind and her curiosity grew as he got them glasses of iced tea.

"Want to come watch me ride?" he asked.

"I don't know about that one. Thank you, though, for the invitation. It all sounds rather primitive," she said and he grinned. "Watching you on a bucking horse—I think it would be frightful."

"I'm glad to hear you'd worry about me. I won't be on a horse. I'm entered in the bull riding."

Aghast, she frowned. "You won't be worth much to Noah if you're in the hospital with broken bones," she said before she thought. She would have never made such a remark to Noah. With Jeff, she didn't care if her annoyance showed, even though she knew she was being unprofessional and overstepping bounds.

He laughed. "Ahh, you're not worrying about my well-being. You're worrying I'll foul up Noah and work. I don't intend to be in the hospital. That isn't why I entered. I expect to win a tidy prize. So, want to come watch?"

She shivered. "Thank you, I think not."

They sat on his patio with light from torches flickering and pool lights making the water sparkle.

"I have something to discuss with you," Jeff said, pulling a chair close to face her. "I don't know whether or not Noah has ever mentioned that our father meddles in our lives."

"No, he hasn't," she said, thinking Noah was far too professional to discuss any such thing. "Your father seems to be a strong influence, at least in Noah's life."

"That's right. Much more in Noah's life than mine. That's one reason I love the ranch—the ranch gets me off Dad's radar. But he never stops trying to control the world around him. He's got a proposition for me. Did you know that he offered both Noah and me a million dollars last year if we married during the year?"

Shocked, she stared at Jeff. "No, I think Noah's in love—"

"Noah is in love, but that wasn't why he married," Jeff added quickly. "He actually did fall in love with Faith."

"I'm certain he did. It was rather obvious."

"Well, the year came and went and I didn't marry and it's worrying my dad. He's made me another offer. If I marry *this* year, I get the family ranch. It's all mine as of the time I marry. He'll balance the inheritance for Noah in cash."

"Do you want the family ranch?" she asked, wondering why he wanted to tell her this because it was none of her business. She knew he was getting to something. If he had asked someone to marry him, it would make a change in their business arrangement.

"Badly," he admitted.

"I can't imagine, though it does make sense. Noah's spoken well of it."

"I want that ranch. I have to marry to get the ranch and the marriage has to last at least a year. He never mentioned children. That's it."

She looked into Jeff's eyes and suddenly knew where he was going. "No!" she exclaimed without realizing she had said a word.

He placed his hand caressingly on her nape, distracting her as her heart jumped. "Marry me, Holly, for one year."

She opened her mouth to protest and he placed his finger lightly on her lips, silencing her. "Listen to me. I've thought about this. Here's what I can offer you in return—"

She twisted her head away. "No! Absolutely not. It's ridiculous. I don't want to hear your plans. I'm not marrying you and living out here on this prairie with the buzzards and rattlesnakes and cows. Never. You can stop now. There is nothing that will change my mind."

"Maybe," he said calmly, still caressing her nape and disturbing her even more. "You can hear my proposal. Marry me for the one year. That's not a lifetime. A million dollars to you and I'll set you up in your own business when the time is up. You're smart and ambitious and capable of running a business. Why not have your own? I know you don't mind the work."

Stunned, she stared at him while his offer buzzed in her thoughts. One million dollars plus her own business in exchange for one year married to Jeff. *No* was still on the tip of her tongue, but she couldn't say it. She had to give his offer some thought. One year wasn't a lifetime, as he had said. She would be working for him and staying on the ranch for a year anyway. A million dollars in addition to the fantastic amount she would get from Noah, plus setting her up in her own business. She didn't have to get buried on this ranch. It was temporary.

Marriage without love. Could she tolerate that? The thought of sex with him made her heart race.

"You think it over. I know you're shocked. Marriage looks feasible to me."

"You'll be going into this marriage knowing it is fake and temporary."

His smoky eyes were wide and direct. "Yes, and so would you. But we both stand to gain a lot. And it should be bearable. There's no man in your life right now."

"No, there isn't and won't be anytime soon no matter what we do."

Dazed, she stared at him, thoughts swirling over his offer and then the moment changed. Jeff had been close, his knees lightly touching hers.

When his hand slipped beneath her chin, tilting her face up as his gaze lowered to her mouth, she quivered in anticipation. Her lips parted as she leaned toward him and then his mouth covered hers. Her heart thudded when his tongue went in her mouth and he lifted her to his lap easily. He shifted her against his shoulder as he kissed her, a steamy kiss that made her forget the negatives concerning him.

She wound her arms around his neck, running her fingers through his thick, short hair, kissing him passionately in return. His kisses melted her, heated her in a manner no one ever had before. She moaned softly, the sound muffled by their kisses.

He was aroused, shifting her slightly to hold her closer. He caressed her throat and his hand slipped lower to caress her breast. Through her clothing, she could feel his scalding touch that heightened her longing.

After twisting free the top buttons on his shirt to slip her hand beneath to his bare chest, she tangled her fingers in the mat of chest hair.

He had unfastened her blouse, the clasp on her bra, cupping her breast as his thumb drew lazy circles. Sensations rocked her and she realized they were going faster than she'd intended.

With an effort, she sat up. His hair was tousled, his mouth red from kisses and his eyes filled with desire. He looked down, cupping her breasts. She gasped with pleasure as he caressed her.

"We have to stop now," she whispered, more to herself than him. She opened her eyes to shift away and stand, trying to straighten her clothes, struggling for a moment to get herself composed. She longed to go back into his embrace, but she knew she would regret it later.

She returned to her chair. "Things got out of hand quickly," she said.

He studied her with a concentrated look that made her wonder what he was thinking. "Marriage should work," he said. "We can do this and both come out better off. Neither of us will be hurt when we break it off."

"It would mean I'd live here on the ranch for a year," she said, viewing that prospect as a calamity.

He grinned and leaned forward to touch her chin. "Brace up. For one million and your own business, it should be worth it and my house is rather comfortable. As it is, you're here during the week."

She blushed with embarrassment, realizing how she had sounded about his home. "Sorry, Jeff, but I have my condo and my friends in the city. I'll have to give your proposal some thought. There are some huge drawbacks. The slim chance of a pregnancy, for example."

"You know as well as I do there are ways to avoid that. We'll be careful."

"I'll have to give this some thought. Right now, it seems ridiculous to even attempt."

"Not at all. You think about it. We're compatible. We've already found that out."

"It's getting late. I'll turn in, but I don't think I'll sleep." She stood and he came to his feet, gathering up their glasses to carry them inside.

They talked about possibilities as they headed to their rooms. At her door, he stretched his arm out against the doorjamb, leaning close while he touched her hair lightly. "I think this is the perfect solution for both of us. All you have to do is say yes and we're on our way."

She looked into wide eyes that could play havoc with her thought processes and her life. "I'll think it over," she repeated breathlessly, recalling his kisses. She reached for the door and stepped inside her room. "'Night, Jeff."

He smiled at her. "See you in the morning."

She closed the door and crossed the room, stopping to look at herself in the mirror. Her hair was down, slightly disheveled, her mouth still red from his kisses. Her flushed face reflected her excitement, passion, his proposal. From the moment he had come into her life he had been a whirlwind of change in every aspect of it.

She was already living in West Texas, out on his ranch, working in a remote office with a man who might live up to expectations and might not.

If she accepted his proposal, she worried it would be too easy to lose herself in him. He hadn't proven anything yet about his abilities. What kind of man was he to have being a cowboy as his prime goal in life? He was far too laid-back for her. There were many stumbling blocks in his plan.

A million dollars, in addition to what Noah was giving her, plus Jeff setting her up in her own business if she wanted him to. She had always dreamed of having her own wholesale accessory line. She knew the business and would know how to run one. She could shape it after the structure of Brand Enterprises. If she had the right products. She had the contacts, the experience. What she needed was money. The prospect was dazzling. She would be comfortable for life and could do as she pleased.

Could Jeff live with her for a year without growing tired? She didn't know him well enough to know how he would react. He seemed too easygoing to take relationships seriously, even with the ranch at stake. She had seen some of the women who came over to their table to flirt and talk with him. They had touched him casually, but with the kind of touch that indicated they might have had a physical relationship before. She suspected he'd had a lot of shallow relationships, but she knew she was guessing.

The moment she thought about accepting, disaster seemed to loom. Yet if she turned him down, without a doubt he would find someone else and she would see what she could have had lost forever.

With her thoughts and emotions in turmoil, she got into bed, staring into the dark while she mulled over her future. He wasn't in a huge hurry for her answer, but she couldn't go to sleep and put his proposal out of mind. It would be a monumental change in her life.

Her family would take it in stride and probably understand her reason for acceptance, since any of them would do the same. Each member of her family was ambitious, money-hungry, determined to continue achieving success, so they would tell her to accept if she asked anyone's advice. As far as Jeff's relationship with them was concerned, he could charm people and he seemed to have a wide circle of friends. Even in Dallas at the office, she'd been surprised by the number of men who stopped to talk to him and welcome him back, greeting him warmly and seeming sincerely interested in what he was doing.

Returning to Dallas Friday for the weekend, she tried to get some normalcy into her life.

As they ate salads Sunday evening, Holly told Alexa about Jeff Brand's proposal. Alexa lowered her fork to her plate and stared wide-eyed at Holly. "A million dollars and your own business? That's a fabulous offer."

"Alexa, if I accept, I marry him. Tied to Jeff in marriage. That's a close, intimate relationship. I have uncertain, negative feelings where he's concerned. I don't even know him that well."

Alexa frowned. "That's too big an offer to turn it down."

"Perhaps. I really have to give it thought."

"One year, Holly. You're not thinking straight on this. Stop hesitating. Jump at this golden opportunity."

Alexa frowned again, tapping her fork on her plate. "You're out there with him for a year anyway. If he's sexy—I assume charm also includes sexy?"

"Yes," Holly answered.

"If you're there one year anyway and he's appealing, you might fall in love with him and not get the million, the marriage or have him set you up in business."

"There are drawbacks either way I go. Just which way will be the most livable."

"There, you see? The most livable is getting the million dollars. End of argument."

Holly smiled. "I think you're overlooking some important points, but I'll keep this conversation in mind."

"I'll try to avoid saying 'I told you so' if you don't accept."

"I will appreciate that," Holly replied in amusement. "Each time I decide to say yes, I get scared to pieces about what I'm committing to doing."

"If you marry, I'm going to miss you here."

"Whatever happens, I'm not giving up this condo. That palace Jeff lives in is ridiculous. I want a place I can come stay when I'm in Dallas—and I will be in Dallas, whatever happens."

"Most women would jump at the chance to live in a palace."

"You should see it. I've seen hotels that are smaller. No, I'll still be your neighbor, just not here as often."

She and Alexa parted at the doors of their condos. She wanted some time to herself. All weekend she had weighed both sides of Jeff's proposition and she was beginning to lean toward accepting. It was too big to turn down.

Money flowed at that ranch with every luxury possible. Mrs. Jeff Brand. She couldn't imagine being married to him. They barely knew each other. In reality, there was the possibility she would be in his bed before the year was out, married or not, so she might as well go for the deal he offered.

Making her decision, she discarded negative thinking, holding on instead to the possibilities.

Jeff was out of the office Monday to attend a business meeting with Noah and she didn't see him until the next day at the ranch. It was half past eight when he appeared at the door of her office. "Morning. Have a nice weekend?"

"Yes. And you?" she asked, barely thinking about

his answer as she studied him. Dressed in his usual jeans and Western shirt and boots, he looked more cowboy than the billionaire rancher he was. Yet her pulse raced and she stared at him, thinking soon she might be his wife. She realized he noticed the intensity of her gaze.

"I'm sorry. My mind was on some figures I'd been going over," she said, flustered and trying to cover her lapse.

"I just said that I wish you'd contact Garrett Linscott and see if you can get me a telephone appointment with him. I don't want to leave this to one of the secretaries because you might be able to talk him into it."

Surprised by his request, she nodded. "I'll try, but he's very cool to Noah and vice versa. Noah has little to do with Garrett Linscott."

"We never could work out the dollars with them. They always wanted more profit than anyone else. Too much for Dad, certainly. I'd guess Garrett has snubbed Noah, who simply brushed him off and went on to other accounts, but that's one of the most prosperous Southwestern clothing chains. I rode in a rodeo with Garrett years ago. See if he'll talk to me."

"I'll try," she said and Jeff walked away.

She got the phone appointment and forgot about it until the afternoon when Jeff again walked into her office and sat across the desk. "Thanks for getting Garrett for me. I figured you could. I'm having dinner with him this Thursday."

"Where?" she asked, knowing Garrett Linscott lived in Houston.

"In Houston. I'll fly down. Holly, I'd like you to go with me."

Surprised, she nodded.

"Great," he said, unfolding from the chair and standing. "We'll leave that morning so we don't have to rush. I'll get Nita to make the reservations for our hotel rooms and a limo. We'll come back Friday."

"Sounds fine," she said. "What's the purpose of this dinner? I assume you'll try to get them to carry Brand products."

"No. I want to get him to carry the Cabrera line. Which is Brand's in a way, but not under the Brand name."

"They've been extremely unreceptive—I don't know how much difference a ride in a rodeo would make when it comes to business."

"The rodeo was years ago. What will make the difference is the Cabrera line itself. We'll see. At least he's going to meet with me and talk to me."

"True. We've made headway where Noah and your dad couldn't," she said. It should be an…interesting evening though she brightened at the prospect of dinner in Houston.

All through the day she could barely concentrate on business with Jeff's proposal on her mind.

By five o'clock she found it impossible to think about business and she was thankful when she heard the secretaries leave. Jeff appeared soon afterward.

"Why don't you quit early tonight? We can swim and then have dinner."

"I'm ready," she answered. "I'll meet you in front in a few minutes," she said as she turned off her computer.

Nervousness churned in her because it was answer time. All day he had been his usual, casual self with nothing to hark back to his proposal of last week. Yet she knew the subject would come up this evening. The closer she approached to giving him an answer, the more nervous she grew about it.

She stepped out of the office into another blast of heat. He took her arm and led her to his car. "We'll drive. It's quicker."

They talked about the day and still nothing about the proposal that loomed all important in her mind.

She moved as if on autopilot, swimming with him and then changing for dinner while most of her thoughts were on the one burning subject. After swimming, she dressed in white linen slacks and a matching blouse, and every time she considered turning him down, she knew she didn't want to. She combed her hair out, letting it fall loosely across her shoulders. Her determination to stick by her decision to accept grew.

Finally she went outside to find him. The table was set with a large bouquet of daisies and roses. Wine was chilled. Jeff had changed and she drew a deep breath as she approached him. "Ready for a glass of wine?"

"Yes, please," she replied, aware of his appreciative gaze.

"I hope we're going to have a celebration dinner," he said as he handed her a glass of pale liquid.

"Here's to the future, Holly," he said, standing close and raising his glass in a toast. "Are you ready to give me your answer?"

Five

She raised her glass to touch his lightly and then sipped the chilled dry wine.

He set his glass on a table and took hers from her, taking her into his arms. "Well, what's it going to be? Will you accept my proposal? Will you marry me?"

"I've been thinking about it, Jeff. Let's talk about terms."

"Ahh," he said, amusement lighting his eyes.

Her heart drummed. "You've offered me a million dollars and to set me up in business. The offer to set me up in business is too vague. What would that involve? You have to have a limit."

"Practical Holly," he teased, tugging a lock of her auburn hair lightly. "We'll set a limit on my part at one million dollars. How's that? You'll have money of your own to put into it."

She nodded. "Fair enough. You want marriage for a

year. You've offered a million plus the business. I'd like another half million because this ties me to the ranch far beyond this job. That means one and a half million cash plus the other incentives, but I imagine you'll be gaining far more than that."

"That's true, Holly. Okay," he said, surprising her at his quick agreement, making her wonder just how much money Jeff was worth. "Do we have a deal? Will you marry me?"

"This is crazy. Yes, I will," she replied. The amount of money she would be getting dazzled her.

With a whoop, he swung her in the air, spinning around to make her laugh while she held his shoulders. As he swung her around, she felt his muscles flex. Lowering her, he held her close. "Holly, we'll be all right. You'll see. We'll each get what we want. First, though, let's do this right," he said and his mouth covered hers as he leaned down to kiss her.

When he drew her closer, her heart thudded as he kissed her, stroking her tongue with his, sealing their promise to each other with the passion he had talked about.

He would soon be her husband. She poured herself into their kiss. Yet as passion built, she finally stopped. "Jeff, we have so many decisions to make." He straightened up and released her slightly. Both of them were breathing hard, their hearts pounding.

"You just made the big one. You won't regret it. Besides, the year will be gone in no time," he added with a smile. "Ahh, Holly, this is good. We'll have a fine agreement. I'll get my lawyer to draw up a prenuptial agreement and you can get your own lawyer to look it over."

"I would like that," she said, knowing she could now afford to do such a thing. "This is still crazy, Jeff."

"Not so crazy for what we each get out of it."

"I suppose we're going to present ourselves to the world as in love since you have to do so for your family."

"Yep, although Noah will know better. He knows how you felt about coming out here."

"My family is so busy, they'll accept what we say and go on with their lives, so no problems there. I've already told one of my closest friends."

"It won't matter. Dad told Noah to just pick some woman he was compatible with and get married."

"I knew your dad had the final say with everything in the company, but I didn't know he was that determined to get what he wanted," she said, beginning to understand a little of Jeff's rebellion.

"Wait a minute." Jeff left the room abruptly and when he returned held out a box wrapped in shiny gold paper. "This is for you, Holly." She opened it to find another box and then a black velvet box that she opened. Her breath caught at the dazzling diamond ring flanked by smaller diamonds.

"Jeff, this is gorgeous!" She glanced up at him. Guilt struck her for demanding another half million from him.

"Let's see if we got the size right," he said, taking it from her and slipping it on her finger.

"It's perfect. How'd you know?"

"Lucky guess."

"This is the most beautiful ring I've ever seen," she said, shaken by the commitment she had just made.

"I think maybe I've rushed into this too fast," she

whispered, thinking aloud. "Jeff, if you do things like this for me, you forget the half million I asked for."

He hugged her. "You might make it worth my while."

She looked up at him, slipping her arm around his neck. "Thank you. This is way beyond anything I dreamed," she said. She stood on tiptoe to kiss him.

His arm went around her waist and he held her tightly as he leaned down to kiss her in return.

Her heart pounded with desire. She spun away in his scalding kiss as she kissed him with eagerness.

While his fingers wound in her hair, he kissed her. She ran her fingers through his hair and then down his muscled back, wanting him physically, on fire with the need to love him.

She looked up at him to find him watching her. "Let's set a date soon. The sooner we marry, the sooner the year begins."

"I can't stop looking at my ring," she said, wiggling her fingers. "Jeff, this is so extravagant, it's sinful."

"Not really. Who knows, Holly? This may be the only time in my life I marry. I might as well do it as right as I can."

"I hope it isn't the only time either of us marries," she said solemnly, unable to imagine this marriage would last.

"We don't have to worry about that now. Holly, I'll pay for the wedding and you can do whatever you want, so don't let money hold anything back. If you can have this wedding soon, we'll manage to get it done," he urged, reaching over to toy with a lock of her hair. His warm fingers brushed her nape and it was difficult to concentrate on a calendar. She tried to think about her own appointments. Jeff had his all marked in the calendar he handed her.

She looked at it and for a moment was dazed, unable to focus. Everything was happening sooner than she had anticipated.

"If I can get things done quickly, it'll cost more." He waved his hand and she continued, "I can get married the third weekend of August."

"Done. The third weekend in August. Let's go see my family to tell them. I'll call and ask all of them to dinner tomorrow evening, telling them I have a friend I want them to meet. That should be a red-flag warning. We'll meet them in Dallas. My mom will want to meet you anyway. You watch. They will want to have an announcement party for us soon."

"Your mother never came to the office. I never did see her at company events. I would feel guilty about this except you told me your dad told Noah to just marry someone compatible in order to be married. That's callous."

"Nope. It's Dad wanting to get his way." Jeff crossed to the table to get a cordless phone that he put on speaker. She listened as he made calls and arranged for dinner with his family.

She couldn't keep from continually looking at her ring, which was dazzling, and she wondered how long it would take her to get accustomed to it. She glanced at Jeff as he talked, her heart skipping. He was going to marry her and shower a fortune on her. One year was all that was required of her. The uncertainties she felt about Jeff would be gone out of her life in a year. She had mixed feelings about the turn her life had taken. Exciting, beyond her wildest dreams while at the same time, she would have a close relationship with a man she would never have selected on her own.

In August she would be his wife. The thought stirred fluttering inside her. Mrs. Jeff Brand. She looked at him again, remembering how he had looked in the pool almost naked—lean, muscled, sexy.

He finished his calls and turned to her. "We're set. Meet them at the club tomorrow night at seven. We'll shut down early from work. We can go ahead and announce it at the office and you can show off your ring. I'm going to call Uncle Shelby and invite him, just in case he's in the country."

"Nita and Daphne will hate me. They love flirting with you."

He shook his head. "I've tried to ignore that. It should go away now."

"They are going to be crushed."

"Then after the office formalities, we'll have a party so I can introduce you to the cowboys who work on the ranch, my foreman and local friends. We'll invite Nita and Daphne and they'll meet guys who will interest them far more than I have."

"That I doubt," she remarked. "We better start getting dates down on the calendar."

"What kind of honeymoon do you want?" He walked over to her to take her into his arms and kiss her. It was another half hour before she ended their kisses.

"Jeff. Wait. Not so fast." She straightened her clothes, trying to get herself composed. "Let's call my family. They'll be surprised, but that's about all there will be to it. They lead busy lives and are all wrapped up in what they are doing."

It was an hour before they finished talking with her parents and her brothers. The more time that passed, the

more she felt anxiety crowding her over this marriage
that neither of them really wanted. She noticed that Jeff
had grown quieter. She suspected his own anxiety level
was climbing. Each call was more binding, reaffirming
the reality of marrying. "We might as well sit down and
start making wedding plans because neither of us will
sleep."

It was almost three in the morning when she told
him good-night.

Her uncertainties grew. She reminded herself that
the commitment was only for one year. The last thing
before she switched off a bedside light was a long look
at her new ring while she thought about Jeff's kisses.

The next day, Jeff shut himself in his office and
called Noah.

"I want to talk—do we need to make an appointment?"

"No. I have a meeting later this morning. I'll see you
tonight. What's up that you want to talk now?"

"I want you to know before tonight. Are you sitting
down?"

"Don't tell me you're quitting."

"No. Far from it. I'm getting married, Noah."

"Wait while I pick myself up off the floor. Who's the
lucky bride? I remember Carrie, Emma, Polly—I'm sure
there are plenty I don't know. How'd she talk you into
it?"

Jeff laughed. "She didn't. Remember Dad's deal
about the ranch if I marry?"

"I'll be damned. You've proposed to someone. Oh,
hell. You aren't doing this only because of the offer Dad
made to you about the ranch? Not you."

"Afraid so. That's why I wanted to tell you now.
We're telling the world we're in love."

"Don't just marry to get the ranch. I can't even believe I'm saying this to you. You of all people. You've always been able to resist Dad's prizes and his manipulations. Does your fiancée have a clue that you're not wildly in love with her?"

"She knows it because I've made a bargain with her. A damn big bargain."

There was a long silence finally broken by Noah's swearing. Jeff could imagine his brother's scowl. "Dammit, Jeff. It's not Holly, is it?"

"Yep. You bribed her, so I figured I could, too."

"I expected to get her back, you realize. She's one of my best employees."

"You still might someday. We've made a deal we're both happy with."

"I can't imagine. You must have paid her a colossal amount of money. She'll be too independent to work for me. You two don't even like each other. Why are you locking yourself into that kind of situation?"

"We'll manage. There are moments when we get along," Jeff remarked dryly, thinking about kissing her last night and wanting her now. "I'm paying her a mil and a half. Up front. She'll make way more than that, but that's the big incentive. I've already given her a diamond like a headlight."

"Don't do this. You'll regret it. I can't even believe we're having this conversation. I'm saying to you what you've said to me all my life."

"And you've benefited far more from Dad's generous rewards for doing what he wants than I ever have. Well, brother, I've finally wised up and will reap my bounty."

"I would have bet the house that she would turn you down. Of course, over a million—she's ambitious."

"I've offered her a few other perks, as well," Jeff said, avoiding breaking the news to Noah about his business offer.

"You're making a mistake. You're way too much a free spirit and you have too many women friends to settle into any kind of relationship with Holly unless you two simply live under the same roof and go your separate ways. I guess I'll stop talking. You've already done what you wanted to do, but that family ranch isn't worth getting tied into marriage with someone you're at swords' points with."

"I want the damn ranch. I think we can do this and if we can't, we'll get out of it."

"You get out of it within a year and Dad will raise hell over giving you the ranch. Or is that what you intend?"

"Nope. To most outsiders, we'll look like a couple in love. She's going to tell her closest friends and her family because they're driven with ambition, too, from what she's told me. She seems to think they'll understand."

"I have that same impression. I've never met them. I don't think she sees them often. Now I'm sorry I had her work for you. I don't think this will do either of you any good."

"Stop being so negative. We're adults and we're doing what we want. She gets almost two million and I get the ranch. That's not a bad trade-off."

"It would be to me. I hope you can still say that a year from now." Noah sighed loudly. "All right, you're engaged I assume."

"And we'll have a wedding soon. I want to take you and Faith and the folks to dinner with us tonight if possible and we'll announce this. You can tell Faith everything as far as I'm concerned."

"Sure. We're free tonight."

"I'll call the folks and call you back. Cheer up, Noah. We're of age."

Noah snorted. "For all that you act like it. I'll still be in shock tonight. I won't tell Faith until later. That way her reaction will be better."

"Thanks. We're meeting at the club at half-past six," Jeff said and ended the call.

It only took a few minutes to set up the dinner date with his uncle, who agreed to fly in for it since he was already in Chicago. Jeff left his office to go to Holly's.

Would they be able to tolerate each other for an entire year? Would he be able to settle down and stick with her for that time?

Big unknowns to which he could only guess the answers. He knew what he hoped. His mansion was huge and they could stay out of each other's way. Thoughts of the ranch replaced worries. It was a first-rate cattle ranch with abundant water and a great climate and location.

Shoving back his chair, he went to her office, stepped inside and closed the door. Wide-eyed, she looked up. In slacks and a shirt that was buttoned to her chin, she looked her usual cool self and mildly annoyed by the interruption. He wanted to pull down her hair and take her into his arms.

"I've already told Nita and Daphne that we're closing early. Let's go to the house and get ready. I've told Noah our plans, but he's not telling Faith yet."

"I doubt if he was happy to hear the news. He knows we're not in love."

"You're right. Also, I called Uncle Shelby and told him I was taking the family to dinner to make an announcement. I had to track him down—he's in Chicago, so he's flying down in a private jet to join us tonight."

"Did you tell him the truth about our engagement?"

"No, not yet. I will, but tonight with Dad around, I want everything harmonious and peaceful, so I haven't yet."

"You're close with your uncle, aren't you?"

"More than my dad," Jeff replied.

She dropped her pen and gazed beyond him with a slight frown. Shaking her head, her attention came back to him. "All right. Give me fifteen minutes to wind up what I'm doing."

He nodded and left, suspecting she was having second thoughts about her acceptance.

All he had to do was think about the ranch and he was satisfied. The year would pass and he thought he could get a warmer response out of Holly. If he didn't, could he live with her frosty remoteness? He thought he could. He remembered last night—there had been no coolness from her then.

His usual optimism set in and he returned to his office, wishing she would close and they could go.

That evening, nervousness over announcing their engagement gripped her. Holly stared at the empty doorway. Doubts had assailed her all day and she had looked at her ring over a hundred times she was certain, viewing it as a promise of the money to come from their deal.

When they entered the country club, she still had butterflies in her stomach. Moisture clung to her palms.

"Smile. You look as if you're headed for a disaster."

She glanced up at him. "I feel guilty and I don't know why."

"No need to feel guilty. We're doing what Dad wants."

"Even though I simply told my folks that this is a marriage of convenience, I didn't feel guilty with them. My brothers—my whole family—are wound up in their careers, so they are thrilled over the money I'll get."

"Dad will be happy," he told her, taking her arm. "You look gorgeous tonight."

"Thank you," she answered, suspecting he would have given her the compliment if she'd appeared a wreck. She smoothed the skirt to her sleeveless black dress. "When you and Noah want something, you go after it with all your being. That's one place you're alike."

"I suppose. We get that from Dad. It's all we've ever known."

She greeted Noah, Shelby and Knox. She knew all of them would be friendly, but it didn't help her relax. "Your dad is an older version of you and Noah."

"We've been told that."

She greeted Faith, whom she hadn't seen since their wedding. Noah shook her hand warmly, gazing at her with a smile that never reached his eyes. And then she greeted the senior Brands.

Within minutes Noah's and Jeff's charm had her relatively at ease. She knew Jeff's mother, Monica, was making an effort to be friendly. Soon the women were conversing.

They had a lounge to themselves for cocktails and Jeff

stood at one point. "I want to make an announcement."
He took her hand to draw her to her feet beside him.

"I've asked Holly to marry me."

The family seemed to explode and surround her to
welcome her and to look at the ring that had been in
Jeff's pocket until a few moments ago when he had
slipped it back on her finger. Noah was the last and he
was quiet as he squeezed her shoulder lightly.

"Welcome to the Brand family," he said.

She gazed up at him and while he smiled, she knew
Noah well enough to know that he was less than pleased
with her engagement to Jeff.

Shelby walked over to give her best wishes. He shook
his head. "I can't believe Jeff is marrying. You worked
a miracle."

She smiled. "I'm thrilled beyond measure. Thanks
for being here tonight. It means a lot to Jeff. He feels
very close to you."

"There's always been friction between my brother
and me. A little between the boys. Of course, Jeff and
Noah aren't boys any longer, but I still think of them
that way. They're closer than Knox and I are and I'm
glad. Knox and I have had some bitter moments. I've
never liked the way he favored Noah, but then Noah is
so much like Knox. It's easy for me to favor Jeff because
he's far more the way I am and frankly, he was more
fun to have around as a kid. Jeff was always ready for
a good time.

"Sorry. My family gets along—when we see each
other," she added with a smile.

"I'll look forward to meeting them. They will come
to the wedding, won't they?"

"Oh, yes. We get together a few times a year."

"I take it there are no grandchildren. That draws

families together fast. I've never been as close to Noah as Jeff, but now Erin is a little doll and I'll admit I'm making more trips to Texas just to see her."

"Talking about me?" Jeff asked as he walked up to join them.

"Fascinating subject though you are, we've managed to move on to Erin," Shelby answered, and Holly stood quietly enjoying the conversation as uncle and nephew talked, clearly revealing the closeness of their relationship.

Through dinner, she tried to focus on the conversations. She hadn't wanted any kind of relationship with a man and now she was going into the most intimate one possible.

By the end of the evening Jeff's parents had already planned a party Friday night to announce their engagement to close family friends.

When she climbed into the limo with Jeff and they started back to the ranch, her head was pounding.

"My folks are delighted," Jeff said. "You did great tonight."

"Maybe, but I don't feel like it. Jeff, this is so crazy. I didn't even want any kind of relationship whatsoever. That wedding is going to be here before we know it."

He laughed. "Holly, not one woman in my life has taken such a dim view of me as you do. It's a good thing I've had a lot of female friends or my ego would be demolished."

"That's impossible. You and Noah are both far too sure of yourselves," she remarked. "I'm going to take a week off to get ready for this wedding."

"Fine. Don't forget about Thursday. You're going with me to Houston."

"I'll do that whether I work most of next week or not. Noah is unhappy about our engagement."

"I thought he covered it pretty well."

"You two have talked about it."

"You'd think Noah would have been the one for the marriage of convenience and I would have been the one impetuously in love. Instead, it's the other way around." He glanced at her. "Stop worrying. We'll take things one day at a time."

"I know you're right about focusing on the one day, but this is a big step, Jeff, and we're less than compatible."

"We'll both try because it benefits each of us, Holly."

She knew he was right, but her uncertain future made it impossible to drop her worrying. Jeff's optimism wasn't helping her. It only emphasized how lightly he took life and the future.

If she concentrated more on work, perhaps the marriage jitters would diminish.

Thursday, she had a running current of excitement as she dressed to leave with him for Houston. They had separate suites booked at the hotel and they were having dinner with the president and marketing manager of Linscott Way West stores.

They flew in Jeff's private jet. On the flight and the ride to the hotel, Jeff was relaxed, unconcerned with anything connected with business. Several times, she picked up the portfolio she had about the Linscott stores, hoping to familiarize Jeff and herself about it, but Jeff changed the subject swiftly and twice, he took it from her hands, closing it and setting it aside.

"Don't you want to know about their company so you

can talk to them with some background and knowledge about them?"

"I know about their company. That's why we're flying down here. They have very profitable stores. Stop worrying and enjoy yourself."

She tried to bank her annoyance with him, thinking how Noah would sit and pour over his notes before meetings with people who were new to him.

"Do you ever take anything seriously?" she snapped, wondering why Jeff was making the effort to talk to them when he wasn't prepared.

She saw the twinkle in his eyes and it heightened her aggravation with him.

"Sure, I take lots of things seriously." He trailed his fingers lightly along her cheek. "When we kiss, I take it as vital."

"Jeff, you can be businesslike now," she complained.

"I'm very earnest," he replied and she knew he was teasing her. "Relax, Holly. You don't have to do anything tonight except be your usual charming self and they will be captivated. That's what's important."

"That is not why we're flying across Texas," she stated in exasperation and closed her mouth tightly, turning to look out the window.

"Stop fretting," he said. "Just relax and have a great time."

"That may be impossible," she said, turning to look at him and he smiled.

"We're going to have an excellent dinner and I hope you have a nice evening. I know you're comapring me with Noah."

"He's never as irresponsible and irrepressible," she remarked and Jeff's grin widened.

"I'll try to be as responsible and repressible as possible tonight just for you," he said and she had to smile.

"All right. We'll do this your way. No more business," she declared, giving up on him. If the evening was a fiasco, it would not be her fault.

Six

As she dressed for dinner, her excitement grew. She had bought a new dress for the occasion. A sleeveless dark green that clung to her all above the straight skirt. She put her hair up and stepped into high-heeled sandals. She looked forward to actually seeing Jeff deal with potential clients.

When he knocked on the door of her suite, she picked up her purse and opened the door. "I'm ready," she said, gratified by the pleased expression that greeted her.

"You look gorgeous. You'll dazzle them so much, they won't know what I'm saying anyway." He took her hand and kissed it, an uncharacteristic gesture that charmed her.

"Don't be ridiculous," she said, smiling at him. "You clean up rather well yourself." He took her breath away and she hoped he couldn't feel her racing pulse as he held her arm.

They were driven to an elegant restaurant nestled in tall pines with fountains inside and out.

Once seated in a glassed-in room, she noticed the view of a pool with waterfalls and fountains and blooming lilies. Candlelight and rosebuds in crystal vases were centered on the linen-covered table. With their surroundings easing her disgruntled feelings, she couldn't shake her expectation of a wasted evening. All of a sudden the maître d' appeared with two men, whom Jeff rose to greet—Garrett Linscott and Matt Arapowski.

Jeff was charming over the course of the meal, engaging her in their talk. It didn't surprise her, and she wondered if he hoped to use his renewed friendship with Garrett to get him to be receptive to a sales call from Brand. Noah could be engaging; halfway through dinner, at the latest, he would have brought up some aspect of business.

Over dessert, Jeff sipped ice water and set down his glass. "Garrett, we're carrying the Cabrera boots, saddles and leather goods exclusively."

"I'd heard. That's a coup for you."

"I know you handle the best lines out there, but you don't carry Cabrera in any of your stores."

"No. At one point, it wasn't worth our while to carry them and we've never really bothered looking into it since," he said, glancing at Matt, who gave a negative shake of his head.

Holly sat listening quietly as Jeff talked about what they were missing by not carrying Cabrera. Quoting figures, Jeff covered their margin of profit and the cost-benefit of carrying his boots. Amazed, she saw why he had been amused on the plane. He had a complete grasp of facts and figures.

"You can't get a better boot and they are all hand-tooled by craftsmen," Jeff said. "Right now, Emilio Cabrera himself is still making boots," Jeff said. "Let me send both of you a pair. You wear them and you'll see," he continued. "This is a prestigious line. Looks, feel, wear—they have it all," he continued.

As she listened to him win them over while still entertaining them, she realized she had to quit judging him on appearances and underestimating him. The figures he quoted were some they had gone over when he had been at headquarters in Dallas. From the time they left the office today until now, he hadn't looked at anything as far as she knew, yet he knew cost and pricing and margin—an array of figures necessary to make his pitch.

A couple of times he brought her into the conversation with questions about the line of boots. Yet when Jeff questioned her, she knew he already had the answer, but was merely keeping her in their conversation and doing so without a real break in his sales pitch.

She listened as Garrett and Matt agreed they should try Cabrera boots in their catalog and in certain stores that were their highest-volume stores in high-dollar areas. And then Jeff got back to entertaining them. Looking as if it had been effortless, he had sold them on the boots and they had agreed to carry them, even before getting their gift boots. Realizing he was as sharp as Noah had said, she was astounded. Excitement buzzed in her. Noah would be ecstatic over this sale. He had talked about wanting to try to get Linscott as a customer.

How wrong she had been about Jeff all this time. She hoped her calm facade hid her excitement.

Gradually, she was drawn back into the conversation.

Part of the time Matt chatted with her while Jeff and Garrett reminisced.

When the evening was over, they said their goodbyes outside. After Garrett and Matt had driven away, Jeff summoned their chauffeur. They were soon headed to the hotel.

"Congratulations, Jeff, on a stupendous job tonight. Noah will be overjoyed," she said, feeling excited over the huge sale Jeff had just made.

"Could it be you're surprised?" he asked, smiling at her.

"You amazed me, I'll admit."

Smiling, he leaned close, placing his hands on the seat on either side of her. "You didn't think I was prepared for tonight, did you?"

She could feel her face flush and knew that gave her away no matter how she answered. "I just told you, I was astounded," she repeated, looking into his eyes. He was only inches away. She could detect his aftershave, see the faintest stubble on his jaw. Her heartbeat speeded. "You sold them so easily. You made it look as if there was nothing to it. I know they didn't come prepared to take the Cabrera line in their stores." Her words were breathless and she felt giddy and hot with desire. She wrapped her arms around his neck. "I was impressed," she confessed.

His arm went around her and he lifted her to his lap easily. "Enough about business," he said, leaning closer to kiss her. The instant his mouth covered hers, she forgot the dinner, business, meeting the men from Linscott, everything except Jeff and his kiss.

His hand drifted down her throat, lower over her breast. When she felt his fingers at her zipper, she caught his wrists and leaned away.

"Jeff, we're not even in private right now," she said, scooting off his lap.

"It was an asset to have you along. Thanks, Holly, for providing just the right touch."

"I think you exaggerate, but I'm glad you were happy I was along."

"Before we go back in the morning, do you want to spend a few hours here?"

"I'd love it. There are some things I can look at for the wedding."

"Fine. I'll take you to lunch and then we'll fly home."

The minute they stepped off the elevator at the hotel, he took her arm. "Let me unlock your door," he said, taking her key from her.

The triumph of the evening still simmered and she knew sleep wouldn't occur soon. She wanted to kiss, she guessed, as much as Jeff did.

Jeff opened her door and waited for her to enter. He followed, tossing her key on a table and closing the door, which automatically locked. He turned to pull her into his embrace.

Her heart thudded and she wrapped her arms around his neck, holding him. She kissed him passionately and poured her exuberance from the night into her kiss. He leaned back against the door and pulled her up against him. His erection was hard against her, heightening her own response.

She never felt his fingers on her zipper. Her dress and then her bra fell around her feet. Jeff stepped back and she opened her eyes as he cupped her breasts and caressed her lightly, drawing circles over each taut bud in a sweet torment. Her fingers shook as she pushed away his suit jacket to twist free his shirt buttons.

He paused to pull off his tie and then returned his attention to her, holding her breasts so lightly, his touches feathery, yet scalding.

"You're beautiful," he said in a hoarse whisper.

She pushed his shirt off his shoulders and it fell around his hips, still tucked into his trousers. His broad, muscled shoulders were smooth as she slipped her hands over him lightly. His sculpted chest made her mouth go dry, the sight of him inflaming her desire.

She ran her hands over his chest, tangling her fingers in the thick mat of chest hair, sliding her hands down over his washboard stomach. Without unfastening his trousers, she ran her hands over his thighs and he inhaled deeply, taking her hand to place it on his thick rod.

He unbuckled his belt until she caught his hands.

"We're waiting—remember?" she asked.

He drew another deep breath and ran his hands over her, taking in the sight of her in a lusty look that made her tremble and long to unfasten his belt herself. Yet she wanted to wait, to know him better. Each day opened new doors and she discovered different aspects about him. They weren't in love and were all but strangers. She wanted to feel as if she knew him when she went to bed with him.

"Jeff, wait," she said, wriggling back into her dress and turning. "Zip me, please."

He leaned forward to trail warm kisses on her nape. He showered kisses down her back and her protests died unspoken as she gasped and closed her eyes.

"Jeff!" she whispered, standing still and letting sensations shower her until she turned to pull him close and kiss him.

They kissed, desire becoming roaring flames until

she stepped away and pulled her clothes in place again. "We have to stop tonight. In only a few weeks, we'll be married and then we won't stop or wait."

His ragged breathing was loud. He studied her and reached out to wrap a lock of her hair around her fingers. "I'll be counting the minutes. This will be a good marriage, Holly. You won't regret your decision."

"I hope you're right," she replied solemnly.

"I'll come get you for breakfast. You name the time you want."

"Seven will be fine," she said, trying to catch her breath, too. His hair was a tangle over his forehead, his chest bare. He looked sexier than ever, more desirable. "It won't be long until our wedding," she added, thinking aloud and knowing she would be eager when the time came.

He kissed her lightly and left.

Her heart pounded and she got ready for bed, her thoughts swirling again. The evening had been a glorious victory in the corporate scheme. Who knew what other secrets lurked beneath his facade.

The third weekend in August, she stood in the narthex of the huge Dallas church. Her father held her arm. "You look beautiful today, Holly," Dennis Lombard said in a low voice. "You're still certain about marrying Jeff?"

"Very," she answered firmly, smiling up at her father.

His green eyes were solemn and searching as he looked at her and nodded. "Good. You're making an excellent bargain. With the incomes both of you will have, you should manage well even if it turns out you're less than totally compatible. Marriage is filled with adjustments."

Amused, she listened to the last-minute advice. To her relief, the wedding planner motioned to them. "It's time, Holly, Mr. Lombard."

As trumpets blared and violins began to accompany the organ, they began the walk up the long aisle. She looked at the huge number of guests and then at the eight bridesmaids, with Alexa as maid of honor. Her gaze shifted to the groomsmen. Noah stood beside Jeff as best man. When her gaze met Jeff's, her heartbeat quickened. More handsome than ever in his tux, he gazed back, a faint smile on his face.

She held no doubts now. She was committed and she would be in this marriage for the next year. Tonight they were flying to New York for four days and then on to Paris and she wondered if her excitement was over their enormous undertaking, or if it was the result of knowing she would stay in New York and Paris for the next two weeks.

Two weeks with Jeff on a honeymoon. Her heart raced at the thought. She was astounded that they had filled this huge church with guests. Between each of their families and their sets of friends, the wedding had gotten away from them.

Her father stopped and soon placed her hand in Jeff's warm, callused hand. She gazed into his gray eyes and tingled to her toes.

He smiled and winked at her, making her feel wrapped in a special moment for just the two of them.

They went through the ceremony, repeating their vows and exchanging rings and once she glanced at Noah, who gazed at her impassively, his feelings and thoughts hidden. She wondered whether he still disapproved or had even made one last effort before the wedding to talk Jeff out of going through with it.

Jeff's parents, on the other hand, had seemed to grow more delighted each time she had been with them.

To his glee Jeff's uncle knew the truth about their arrangement. He was overjoyed to see Jeff get the ranch in such a manner.

As she faced Jeff and repeated her vows, mixed feelings besieged her. Handsome, sexy, unpredictable—could she cope with this sham marriage? Jeff was turning out to be what Noah had said—a sharp, savvy businessman, which still astounded her because it seemed effortless on Jeff's part.

He was never rushed, never uptight over deals, never lost in thought about business, yet he was getting things accomplished she had never expected to see happen. Had she completely misjudged him? She still couldn't come to grips with his unorthodox methods.

As she repeated *for better or for worse,* she wondered whether the future would be better or worse. When she contemplated staying on his ranch for a year, she didn't know how she would get through this. Even the money paled when she thought about Jeff's personality and work methods, as well as where she would have to live. That cooled any likelihood of falling in love with him. She would never under any circumstances want to spend her life on his ranch. She clung to the prospect of a honeymoon in New York and Paris and her spirits lifted.

Finally, the minister pronounced them man and wife and introduced them to the guests as Mr. and Mrs. Jeff Brand.

She glanced up at Jeff, who squeezed her hand. They rushed down the aisle into the narthex and around the church to return for pictures as planned. In the deserted hallway, Jeff pulled her close to hug her. "We're married. Thanks for agreeing to this."

"You drive a hard bargain, but I get a trip to New York City," she said, feeling giddy at the prospect.

After pictures, they drove to the country club for the luncheon reception.

She shed the train to her dress and stepped into Jeff's arms for the first dance. "When we get back from the big city, I'll take you to see this ranch I just acquired. Maybe then you'll see why I wanted it so badly."

She doubted if she would. It was simply land with horses and cows and barns and sheds as far as she was concerned. She told him nothing about her feelings; she couldn't imagine he cared how she felt about his home or the ranch he had just received from his dad.

She looked up at Jeff as they circled the floor. "Think we look as if we're a couple in love?"

"Definitely," he replied and she shook her head.

"Ever the optimist. I don't care. My family is happy. Even Noah seems to have accepted this. We have two weeks in two cities."

"Traffic, noise, lines everywhere," he reminded her.

"Restaurants, museums, stores, symphony, opera. People everywhere."

"At least we agree on ribs, and dancing."

"That's about all. Jeff, we're opposites and that's that."

She danced with her father, who seemed pleased for her. As they danced, she saw Jeff with her auburn-haired mother and suspected Jeff would captivate her parents.

Dancing with her brothers, she got the same reaction

as she had with her dad. They all thought she'd made an incredible bargain with Jeff.

She wasn't surprised that the families liked each other because they had a lot in common. Only Jeff with his ranching background was the one who had far less in common with any of them.

It was night when they arrived in New York and she was breathless looking at the city lights.

When they reached the suite of their hotel, Jeff picked her up to carry her inside, setting her on her feet in a luxurious suite that held chilled champagne, lavish hors d'oeuvres, plus huge bouquets of fresh flowers. She crossed the room to the window to look again at the view and the myriad of lights until Jeff turned her to him.

He had shed his suit jacket and tie and kicked off his shoes. He poured two flutes of champagne and brought one to her, turning lights low throughout the suite before he returned to raise his drink in a toast. "Here's to marriage accomplishing what we want."

She laughed and touched his glass lightly with hers. "Jitters come and go. I hope they'll go for good before long."

"Mrs. Jeff Brand. Marriage will be advantageous, Holly."

"Do you always get what you want?"

"Of course not. But I do often enough to be optimistic about life. Another toast," he said, holding out his flute. She watched the pale liquid as bubbles rose to the surface and popped. "No regrets, my love."

"I'll drink to no regrets. The *my love* part is a stretch."

He smiled as they both sipped their champagne. Then he set down his drink and took hers.

The look in his eyes was blatant lust and her heartbeat drummed. He drew her to him. "You were stunning today." He gathered her into his arms. "Mrs. Brand," he said in a husky voice. "First, these have to go," he said, pulling pins out of her hair. Locks tumbled down her shoulders as her heart thudded and she forgot her surroundings and everything except Jeff.

"I don't know how this bargain can work when we're such opposites, but we managed to convince everyone today."

"You try and I'll try and voilà, we should succeed."

All the time he talked, his voice dropped lower, growing huskier. His gaze had shifted from her eyes to her mouth and he slipped one arm around her waist to draw her to him.

Barely able to get her breath, she wanted his kisses, his lovemaking. She had waited, through the past week, dreaming about him at night, fantasizing about this moment when the waiting would be over. She was on the Pill now and they didn't have to worry about a condom.

While she slid her arm around his neck and leaned closer, his mouth covered hers, his tongue going deep. Desire was a flash fire—white-hot and intense—sending her temperature soaring.

Jeff's arm banded her waist tightly as he leaned over her and kissed her hard.

After unzipping her dress, he stepped away to let it fall around her feet. He held her waist, taking his time to look at her. "You're beautiful and you take my breath," he declared in a rasp.

He reached up to unfasten the clasp on her bra.

She sucked in her breath as his hands cupped her breasts. "So beautiful," he repeated, caressing each breast before leaning down to take her nipple in his mouth and run his warm tongue over her.

As she closed her eyes, moaning softly, she clung to his broad shoulders. Tingling from all he was doing, she wanted to drive him wild. She unbuckled his belt and his trousers, pushing them away. He stepped out of them and she pushed away his briefs, freeing him. His rod was thick and ready. She tingled in anticipation.

His marvelous, muscled body, his firm buttocks and long legs turned her desire scalding. He picked her up and carried her in swift strides to the bedroom where he placed her on the bed and then came down beside her to pull her into his embrace.

Writhing beneath his touch, she moaned with plea-sure, wanting more of him and kissing him with all the passion she felt. Desire had been pent-up, their lovemaking limited and cut short from the first kiss. Finally, she could let go and she wanted him with an urgency that shocked her.

Jeff's kisses had always driven her wild. Each time they were together, need and pleasure had heightened. Tonight the barriers between them were gone. Wanting to kiss and explore his strong body, she ran her hands over him. When she pushed him on his back to shower kisses over him, she scooted down to take his thick shaft to caress and kiss.

With a groan, he shifted. She was now on her back and he bent over her, returning kisses and running his hands lightly over her, his fingers traveling down to her legs, caressing her inner thighs.

He caressed her intimately while he kissed her, his

hand moving between her legs, tension spiraling as she arched beneath his touch and cried out. His tongue traveled down over her, showering hot, wet kisses across her belly and then farther, between her legs.

She cried out with pleasure, twisting her hips, unable to keep still, wanting him. She wound her fingers in his hair and thrashed as he drove her wild. Moving her hips frantically, she sat up to pull him to her and kiss him passionately.

"I want you," she cried. "Love me now."

"We're just getting started," he said, starting again to kiss and caress her and then moving down, turning her over to trail kisses down her back, down the backs of her legs as his hand went between her thighs again.

Pleasure was hot, intense and need just as strong. The torment and passion grew as he continued his loving, driving her to the brink.

When he moved between her legs and lowered himself to enter her, she was frantic with wanting him. She tried to pull him closer as he entered her slowly. Hot, thick and hard, he slid into her, then withdrew, setting her on fire. She gasped, tugging him closer with her hands and legs that were wrapped tightly around him.

He entered her again, moving slowly, still maintaining his iron control. He filled her and withdrew. She cried out, arching beneath him, pulling him closer.

"Jeff, come here. I can't wait any longer," she gasped.

"You're passion and fire," he whispered as he pumped and heightened her pleasure.

She ran her hands over him, moving with him, one with him for now.

He finally lost his control and pumped wildly,

sending them both over the brink. She cried out with rapture as she climaxed and then he shuddered with his. Ecstasy enveloped her, swirling her away into brief oblivion.

"Holly, love. Ahh," he gasped.

Slowly, her breathing returned to normal and she began to think and come out of her daze.

Moving together, they held each other tightly. At that moment she felt close to him, as if all differences fell away and were no longer important. She turned her head to kiss him and he kissed her on the mouth in return, a satisfied, loving kiss, light and an affirmation.

Keeping her close with him, Jeff rolled to his side and they lay facing each other.

"You've destroyed me," she said.

"I hope not. That wasn't my intention. Besides, I have plans for you later tonight."

"Don't tell me now," she whispered lazily. "You're a terrific lover. This is your talent, Jeff," she said dreamily, only half aware of talking to him. She was giddy with pleasure. She barely had a sip of the champagne, so she should be cold sober, but his loving had thrust her into a dazed euphoria.

"You're the superb lover, but then I always thought you would be," he replied.

She opened her eyes to look at him. "Always? I think not."

"Maybe not that first day when you were cold enough to give me frostbite, but after our first kiss, I knew."

She laughed softly, thinking even conversation was too much effort. "Ridiculous, but I like hearing you say it."

He chuckled and held her close, stroking her hair. "This is a grand arrangement we have, Holly."

"Beware, neither of us wants to fall in love."

"Not much danger of that I'd say. At this point we do have a spectacular union, though."

She snuggled against him. "What a body you have," she murmured.

"I believe that's my line. Maybe we'll make Paris on the next round and just stay two weeks right here in this hotel room."

Her eyes flew open. "No way, Jeff Brand," she replied. "You promised Paris. We have arrangements—"

"Calm down. I'm teasing, sort of. I'll take you to Paris. But the other was a nice thought."

"If I were a cat now, I would definitely be purring."

He trailed his fingers along her hip and then on her arm. "I can't get enough of touching you or looking at you or kissing you."

"That's good to hear," she replied happily, still in euphoria, enjoying this moment of silly banter with him and the intimacy of the past hour. She felt bonded with him, joined in more ways than purely physical. For the moment, differences dwindled to insignificance. Right now, they weren't poles apart. Tonight they were in harmony and in union.

She knew it wouldn't last, but she cherished it, seeing a side to him she hadn't seen before.

"Jeff, this is a night I'll always remember."

"I hope so," he replied. "Who knows about the future? If it is my only wedding, it's a good one."

"I quite agree," she answered, running her fingers over him. She looked up at him, wondering about him and what in life was deeply important to him beyond being a cowboy. His emotional risks in this marriage

were minimal and she didn't expect him to change.
This was her only wedding night, too. This time their
marriage had been good.

Seven

Congratulating himself on getting her to marry him, Jeff showered light kisses on her temple, ear and throat. He had the ranch and he had Holly in his bed. If the rest of the year was like their first night, he would be in paradise.

At the end of the year, he expected she would be gone instantly, picking up her life where Noah had interrupted it.

He kissed her, his thoughts consumed by desire. He had never been deeply in love or deep in any relationship and he didn't expect that to happen now. He stood and picked her up, carrying her with him to the shower where he set her on her feet and turned warm water on them.

Slowly he began to soap her, running his hands lightly over her, already aroused and wanting her. He was hot, wanting her as if they hadn't just made love only a short time ago.

He moved her beneath the spray to wash off the soap and then turned off the water as he began to kiss and caress her. She was wet, warm, her skin smooth. She moaned softly with pleasure, stirring him more. Her responses heightened his excitement and need and she reacted to each caress and kiss.

"You're beautiful, Holly. So beautiful, love," he whispered, unaware of what he was saying to her as he showered kisses on her throat and breasts. He ran his hands along her shapely legs, caressing between her thighs while she gasped and clung to him.

He shifted, stepping back to brace himself and picked her up, lifting her onto his hard shaft.

She cried out with pleasure, gripping his shoulders and moving on him, setting him ablaze as he thrust into her warm softness, feeling her envelop him. He fought for control, trying to last, to pleasure her until she was wild with passion.

She clung to him with her arm around his neck while her other hand slid over his back and neck, caressing him, heightening his own pleasure.

"Jeff, love me," she gasped, moving on him, and he knew his control was slipping away.

He thrust furiously, moving faster, hearing her sob of pleasure as she held him tightly and shook with her release.

"Jeff." She cried his name as she climaxed and then he reached his, plunging him into ecstasy as he pumped. Shudders of pleasure racked him. His pulse thundered while he soared into oblivion.

Gradually, his breathing returned to normal and he slowed. She was draped over him, stroking his back and showering kisses on his face. He turned his head to kiss her in a long, caring kiss.

"This is great, Holly," he whispered, looking at her. She opened her eyes slowly, a lethargic, satisfied expression, her mouth red from his kisses, her face flushed.

He smiled at her and she smiled in return. He wondered whether there was any danger that after a year with her, he would fall in love. He shrugged away the notion as ridiculous. Whatever he felt at the end of a year, he knew she would be gone instantly. She disliked everything about the ranch—the quiet, the horses, riding, the open spaces. Everything he loved and valued, she rejected.

In the meantime, certainly in the present, he couldn't have done better in choosing a woman for a marriage of convenience.

He shifted, letting her stand to shower briefly. After drying, he picked her up to carry her back to bed where he pulled her close against him, to hold her in his arms.

"Ahh, love, this is the best. I'll show you Paris, but first I want to show you our Parisian bedroom."

"That's fine with me," she replied, shifting to prop her head on her hand and look down at him. "Remember, you made lunch arrangements with your uncle while we're there. He's flying in from London."

"It's our honeymoon. He would understand if I canceled."

"He knows this marriage is a sham and why, so he'll expect you to be able to tear yourself away for a lunch. You'll be glad to see him."

"In the meantime, I will make the most of my time here," Jeff said, suddenly rolling her over beneath him.

She yelped in surprise and then looked up. He saw her green eyes darken slightly with desire, a heated look as she wrapped her arms tightly around him.

As he leaned the last few inches to kiss her, he became aware of every warm inch of her against him. She wound her arms around him and the discussion was over.

It was noon before one of them could even think of breakfast. Holly heard her stomach rumble, and Jeff must have as well because he stretched his long arm and picked up a folder from the table near the bed.

"We'll have room service and eat in the nude in bed."

"I don't know about that. I don't think you'll ever bother with eating if we follow your plan," she said, smiling at him.

"So what if we don't? Hunger will win at some point."

"I veto the nudie breakfast," she said. "You give me time today to check my e-mails. I don't want to lose touch with the office."

"You have got to be joking," he said.

"No, I'm not. We don't need to stay out of total contact. Something vital might happen."

"Holly, you need to learn to relax and enjoy life a bit more."

"I enjoy my life plenty," she said, raising her chin. "I also like to get things accomplished. You might take note."

"I'd rather get back to discussing the nude breakfast. Maybe I can talk you into it. In the meantime, let's order. What would you like?" She found it difficult to concentrate on a menu when Jeff continually kissed and caressed her. It was after one before they finally ordered and breakfast turned into lunch sent to their room.

Over crisp bacon and fluffy scrambled eggs, she stared at Jeff. "Do you realize we've been here four days and never set foot out of the room with this wonderful city filled with all sorts of things to do and to buy?" Mid-morning Thursday they were to leave for Paris.

"I've had a far more entertaining time right here," he answered. "Is this a complaint?"

She blushed. "Not really. You know I've been happy or I would have mentioned this before now. I'm just shocked that neither of us wanted to get out."

"I definitely had something I'd rather have been doing," he said with a grin and she decided to stop talking about getting out of the hotel.

For the next three days, she saw no more of Paris than of New York, but the fourth day, they had that lunch appointment with his uncle and she dressed carefully, excited to see the city.

In a delightful French restaurant they ate outside, and over lunch she enjoyed the surroundings and her food while the men talked. Gradually, as Shelby got to the subject of business, she began to pay more attention to their conversation.

"Jeff, my brother's doctor has told him to get out of the business completely or face dire consequences. Your mom won't and can't do anything with him. She's always left him to do as he pleased and then he leaves her alone to do what she wants. He won't let go, staying on as chairman of the board. I'm busting myself to get more business and I'm glad to see what you did, acquiring the Houston account. I want you and Noah to succeed like crazy because maybe then Knox will step down—if it's not too late."

"Don't run your own blood pressure up doing it. You're not twenty any longer."

"You know me better than that," Shelby said, with good nature.

"Noah will think you're doing it just to show Dad that he isn't necessary because of all your old rivalries."

Shelby shook his head. "Maybe that's part of it. That never dies completely, but age changes us. I don't feel I have to prove anything to Knox. I have a comfortable life. Right now, your dad is overjoyed at the increase in profits. Noah is getting rid of some old accounts that aren't great and making the company more efficient. You've brought in a gem of an account already. It looks good and Knox is pleased."

"I wasn't sure he'd even be happy to see me come back into the business."

"Oh, yes. Is he ever! Especially after the Houston deal. He's plotting ways to keep you in it."

Holly stared at Shelby in horror, thinking there was no way Noah could keep her working for Jeff beyond the year she had agreed to be married to him. Jeff looked as unhappy as she felt as she saw anger flash in his gray eyes.

"No. My agreement with Noah is finite. When this year is up, I'm out of it. There is no deal on earth that will change my feelings about it. I'm not staying in the family business one minute longer than I agreed to." He glanced at Holly. "Holly feels the same. She is less than enthused about working out at my ranch."

Her face flushed as Shelby turned to smile at her. "Surely you find working with Jeff as interesting and rewarding as working with Noah." She knew he was teasing and making light of the whole situation, but she still couldn't joke about it.

"I'm afraid Jeff's right," she said. "I'm definitely a city girl. I can't tell you how much I prefer Dallas to West Texas. When my year is up, I'm heading back to Dallas, wherever I have to work," she said, replying to Shelby, but looking at Jeff the whole time she answered.

Shelby smiled, leaning closer to her and patting her hand. "I can't blame you. I definitely prefer London to Jeff's ranch. That's not the place for me, either. Give me Dallas, Houston, London, Paris. No wide-open country for me."

His attention returned to Jeff. "Just be forewarned. If I hear what Knox decides to do, I'll give you a heads-up, but he has a real knack, as you know, of hitting on the thing someone wants badly. He just did that to you over the family ranch."

"I know, but I can't think of anything he can do to make me stay in this beyond that one year. There's not another ranch and no amount of money would do it. Any change in the Dallas office, Holly will probably know about before I will. She keeps close tabs on the office."

"Enough about business. Holly, what has Jeff shown you of Paris?"

"Not too much," she said, blushing again.

"Then I will remedy that this afternoon, if you'd like. I will take you to see the sights of this beautiful city."

"I'd love it."

Jeff laughed. "So I'll trail along."

"You can do as you please," Shelby said, smiling at her. "I will have a beautiful young woman to show around. You can come along or whatever. She obviously wants to see the sights."

"I do and I'd be delighted for you to give me a tour."

Shelby chuckled. "It looks as if everyone has finished lunch. Shall we get started?"

She had already realized Jeff was not the only light-hearted charmer in the family and she could see why Jeff was so close to their uncle and Noah to their dad. Noah was a carbon copy of Knox as far as she had ever been able to tell when working around both of them. Now Shelby seemed more Jeff's dad than his uncle.

She was entertained all afternoon by Shelby and Jeff, having a delightful time seeing the gems of the city until Shelby paused the group to glance at his watch.

"I will turn this sightseeing over to Jeff. Make him take you places the rest of the day and night so you get a feel for the charm of this city. I have a plane to catch."

"It's been good to see you," Jeff said, hugging his uncle. Never once had she seen Jeff hug his father, yet Jeff and Shelby seemed spontaneous and natural in their warm manner with each other.

"It was delightful," Shelby said, turning to her to take her hand. "You're a wonderful wife for Jeff," he said, looking at her intently. "May your marriage be blessed and continue to grow stronger," he said, giving her a light hug and stepping away.

"Thank you," she answered, puzzled by his parting statement because he knew how temporary and shallow their marriage actually was.

Jeff draped his arm across her shoulders as they stood and watched Shelby flag a cab and climb in to wave farewell to them.

"He makes me want to go out and lose a couple of prime accounts so Dad will get off my back about trying to keep me at Brand beyond the agreed time," Jeff said.

"No. You can't do that to Noah," she said, horrified that Jeff would even jest about such a thing.

"I know and I won't. Noah is innocent in Dad's nefarious schemes. I'm not staying longer and neither are you."

"That's true, Jeff," she replied fervently.

They strolled, stopping on another bridge over the Seine.

"It's beautiful, Jeff," she said, taking pictures until he reached for the camera to snap a picture of her.

As soon as he was finished, she turned to look at the water and the city lining the banks. "This is beautiful. I've dreamed of being here and seeing this, but I always thought it would be so far in the future."

Jeff turned her to face him, placing his hands on the bridge on either side of her. Wind tugged locks of his hair away from his forehead and her pulse skipped as she gazed into his warm gray eyes.

"Now, we can go to another delicious restaurant or we can go to our hotel room and have room service."

"If you'll leave the hotel tomorrow and we can continue sightseeing then, I vote for returning now," she said.

He slipped his arms around her waist. "Here's something else to remember about Paris." He pulled her close and leaned down to kiss her long and passionately.

Locking her arms around him, she returned his kiss, finally hearing someone whistle. She leaned away, looking at him and seeing the desire she felt mirrored in the depths of his gray eyes.

"Hotel room," she whispered.

"Ahh, once again we're on the same page. See, it does happen."

She smiled at him. "Today has been good," she said. "This morning when I checked my calls and e-mails, things were quiet at the office. That's good, too."

"You just can't forget the damn office," he said, shaking his head and smiling.

Whatever the future held, she would never forget Paris with Jeff.

The instant they stepped back into their suite, Jeff kicked the door closed and pulled her into his embrace. Clothes were shed from the door to the bedroom as they kissed and caressed each other and soon he was over her, gazing down with desire blazing in his expression.

They loved through the rest of the day. It took until late afternoon before they finally left their suite for some more sightseeing and a dinner out.

The week passed and she was enveloped in passion, bonding with Jeff and finding a common ground where they could agree often in spite of being opposites in so many ways.

She slept as they flew home over the Atlantic. She was held close against Jeff, dreaming of Parisian nights and rich French pastries.

Flying to West Texas in Jeff's jet over miles of open land, she could feel her reluctance return. She wanted to go home to Dallas, to a city. She reminded herself that she had no choice in the matter. She was now married to Jeff and that changed everything. Their hot nights of passion would make up for some of the drawbacks of the slow pace of life in West Texas.

She turned to look at her handsome husband, reminding herself, as she did daily, to avoid falling in love with him. Jeff was a charmer deluxe. And that meant constantly guarding her heart.

Sunday evening Jeff got a call. She barely listened to Jeff's side of the conversation. Afterward, he turned to her. "One of the cows is calving and having difficulty. I'm going to try to help. It's a great night. Come ride with me in the truck. I don't think I'll be there long."

"Isn't this cow in the barn?"

"Nope. Normally, she would be, but they didn't catch the signs today, so she's in a pasture."

"Sure," Holly said, enjoying his company and not giving much thought to what he was going to do. She stood. "I'm okay in shorts?" she asked, looking at her cutoffs.

"You're gorgeous in shorts," he replied, looking at her bare legs.

"Let's go, cowboy," she said.

They drove with windows down and cool night air blowing in. Beyond a clump of bushes she saw two lanterns set up and two ranch hands bending over a cow.

"There are two men here already. Why do they need you?"

"They probably don't, but I thought I'd check and see how things are going."

"Have you ever delivered a calf before?"

"Yep, I have. If you want, you can sit in the truck—the back of it is out in the open and cool. Or if you'd like, come and I can show you how this is done."

"No thank you," she said, beginning to wonder if she would regret riding along with him. "I'll stay here, but I'll sit outside where it's cooler."

In minutes the men moved away to give Jeff room and Holly had a clear view of him as he put something all over his arm before hunkering down to thrust his arm into the cow.

Holly closed her eyes briefly. She went to the back of the truck to face away from Jeff and the laboring cow. Why he liked working on a ranch, she couldn't imagine.

He stayed until the calf was born. When he wanted to show her the new calf, she had no interest and felt a slight revulsion.

"After checking and helping a little, she had that calf in a normal manner," he said as he started the truck again. "We got a call that a fence is down. On the way home I want to go see if anyone has gone out to fix it yet. You don't mind being a little later getting back, do you?"

"No, I don't," she replied, thankful it wasn't another cow and calf problem. They left the road and bounced over rough ground along a fence row. Finally, two men straightened to face him as beams from the truck headlights splashed over them.

Jeff stopped by to get out and talk. In only minutes he was back in the truck. "They'll take care of the problem here."

"Are there perpetual problems?"

"Sometimes it seems so," he said.

"I absolutely can't fathom why you like this life. It's hard, tedious, sometimes dangerous, out in the elements, physical."

"I think you just listed all the reasons I prefer it," he said. "We're headed home to a fun time now that we can both agree on," he added in a huskier voice.

The next Monday in Dallas, she looked up to see Jeff enter the office. He always wore a business suit to Dallas and he looked handsome and far more professional. The boots were ever present and when he left the office, the Stetson returned to his head, but most of the time here, he looked like a businessman—an enormous improvement as far as she was concerned.

He sat in a chair across from her and stretched out his long legs. "Have a minute?"

"Yes. What's up?"

"I've had a phone call from the president of Western Living. They want to meet with me."

"Jeff, that's wonderful," she said, knowing it was another prestigious line like the Houston line.

"I'll go to Phoenix. I want you to go with me. I think it was an asset to have you along in Houston."

She was flattered and pleased with the prospect of being included. "Thanks. I'd love to."

"Let's take an extra day to stay and enjoy Phoenix."

"I see no point in that," she answered. "That's just goofing off." The minute the words were spoken, she saw amusement flash in his expression. He stood and rocked back on his heels. "R & R. You don't even know what that is or how to do it. Just give it a try. I'll find something that makes Phoenix really interesting and worth your time."

"Whatever, Jeff," she answered, her patience beginning to fray with his casual attitude.

"I'll get the arrangements made and let you know," he said.

She met his gaze and longing stirred as she looked into his eyes. He stood on the other side of her desk, yet she could feel desire, palpable and hot enough to make her breath catch and drive all other thoughts out of mind.

"Another hour and we can leave here. Want to get a hotel room here, eat out and drive home in the morning?"

"I'd love it. I haven't been back to it, but I still have my condo. We can stay there."

"You kept your condo?" he asked, sounding surprised.

"Yes," she replied. "I can afford to now and if I want a place to stay when I'm in Dallas, I have it."

"Good. That's what we'll do. Five o'clock and we're out of here."

She nodded, knowing he wanted the same thing she did. At the moment five sounded a long time in the future, but it was only an hour away. She watched him walk out of the room, remembering their lovemaking of the past night and wanting to be out of the office and in Jeff's arms.

It was impossible to keep her mind on work for the next hour and at half-past four, she began to close up. By a quarter to five, she was ready to go and when Jeff appeared in the doorway, her pulse jumped with eagerness.

"Let's go."

"No argument here," she replied breathlessly, gathering her things and hurrying to join him.

The minute they entered her condo, Jeff pulled her into his arms. Their loving was frantic, even though it hadn't been twenty-four hours since the last time they made love.

Two hours later she was in his arms, sated, lethargic, content. He held her close and when he talked, she could feel the slight rumble in his chest beneath her fingers. "I've thought about you all day. This afternoon, I wasn't worth much as far as work was concerned," he said. He twirled a long lock of her hair around his finger.

"I have to admit to the same problem. This is better now."

"We could have something delivered and stay right here."

"No. You said you'd take me out. We will have to eat at home all week at the ranch. Tonight we go out if you want to win any points with your wife."

"Out it is," he said in a good-natured manner. "Name the place."

"That's risky, you know."

"Go ahead. I'll splurge. Especially if you promise loving again after dinner."

"We'll rush right back here."

"You have a deal," he said, turning her on her side to face him and smiling at her. "This is so very good, Holly. I hope you think so, too."

"There is a limit on this marriage and then it's over."

"You got that right. I'll tell you what, love, I'm never going to live in a city."

She gazed into his wide gray eyes and knew he meant every word, just as she did. "We never planned for this to last. This is a doomed marriage," she said.

"Not doomed, just exactly what we contracted for it to be—temporary. No strings, no heartbreak because no one's heart is involved."

Something hurt deep inside with his words. She knew it was ridiculous to hurt because he was right. Yet he sounded callous and uncaring even though he had described exactly the arrangement they had. Was she guarding her heart—or was that an illusion because Jeff was becoming important to her? Was it sensuality and lust that stirred her constant longing? Or were real feelings beginning to grow for him?

She ran her finger along his jaw, unable to decide what she truly felt, wondering how important he was to her. It was a shock to think that her feelings toward him were changing. She still didn't like so many things about him—his work attitude and methods, that laid-back approach to life, his love of the ranch and horses. Jeff was her total opposite. On the other hand, there were new impressions she had after watching him win clients for the company. She had to admit, there were moments when she had been impressed and her opinions of him had improved. There still couldn't be a danger of falling in love with him.

As he drew her closer to kiss her, she forgot about her worries over the future.

Later that week they flew to Phoenix where they went out with three clients, the CEO and two vice presidents of a prestigious Western store that had outlets in five cities. Jeff got an agreement with them to carry Cabrera products. Later that night when they returned to their hotel suite, he picked her up to swing her around as he let out a jubilant whoop.

Grabbing his shoulders, she shrieked in surprise and then laughed. "Jeff, stop whooping. They'll throw us out of the hotel."

"No, they won't. We're in the most expensive suite they have and believe me, it is expensive, although I could do just as well in a motel because all I want is you and a bed. Tonight was incredible. You're great with these guys and I can tell they're always shocked someone so beautiful knows so much about the facts and figures of the lines. Thanks for coming with me."

"It was a marvelous evening. Jeff, you did an excellent job," she admitted, once again impressed with what he had accomplished. "I wish we were going straight back to the Dallas office. Noah will be jubilant."

"Hey, have you forgotten, we're staying to discover Phoenix? To hell with the Dallas office."

"I'll never understand you," she said, meaning it totally. "How can you be so good at this and at the same time not care at all? You don't care what Noah thinks, or your father's opinion, or even the entire office. I can't understand your attitude."

Becoming somber, he leaned close to look her in the eye. "That's because I don't like the corporate life. That's what you can't understand. That's what you're really married to, Holly. Not me. It's work. You love working. That's the most important thing to you. I guess I get some of that about ranching, but never Brand Enterprises. We'll never be on the same page on that." For a moment there was a tense silence and then she could see the change in his expression as he smiled at her again. "To hell with business. You were wonderful tonight."

Pleased, she held him, leaning forward to kiss him. He let her slide down until her feet were on the floor. She stood returning his kisses until he finally carried her to bed.

The next night when they were back at the ranch, after once again making love, Jeff left her to return and hand her a box tied in a blue silk ribbon. "For you, love."

Surprised, she opened it and was dazzled by a necklace of diamonds.

"Jeff, this is spectacular!" she gasped, unable to believe he had bought it for her.

"I want you to have it," he said, taking it out of the box. "Turn around."

She was astounded Jeff had bought it for her. It was cold against her as he placed it around her neck. She held up her hair and he fastened the clasp.

She turned, going to stand in front of a mirror. She was wrapped in a sheet and the necklace sparkled as the diamonds caught the light. "Jeff, it's fit for royalty. You should not have done this."

"You deserve it," he said. "You helped me twice now with two of the best accounts Brand has."

"You're very good at what you do and you wouldn't have needed me in either case."

"We could argue all night. You take the necklace. It's for you and that's that." He pulled her into his arms to kiss her.

She poured herself into her kiss. Excited, she was still on a high from the business success.

Through the night and the next day they made love.

She was in Jeff's office when Noah called and she could hear Jeff's part of the conversation. She realized Noah was heaping praise on Jeff.

When he ended the call, Jeff looked at her. "You can guess what that was. You should get a call yourself from Noah. To say the least, he's pleased and he's already informed Dad."

"Your dad is going to want you to stay even more."

"Doesn't matter," Jeff answered lightly. "Next weekend, let me show you the ranch I got with this marriage. You've never seen it and I think you'll like it. I want to show you the Brand ranch that had belonged to my grandfather first." When she nodded, he smiled.

"I'll go, but a ranch is a ranch, still cattle and horses and still out in the country," she said with a sigh.

"Let's take Friday off and go. We'll come back through Dallas and stay at your condo."

"Great," she said, actually feeling little enthusiasm.

"Then we'll leave Friday afternoon. Also, I'm riding in a rodeo in Fort Worth soon. Come with me. You might have a good time."

"Jeff, I can't get fired up about a rodeo, but I'll try."

"We make a good team," he replied. For the first time, she began to get edgy at the realization of how much time they were spending together. The first month of the year was almost gone. Eleven more months to go. If they had half the success they already had with new accounts, it would be a phenomenal year.

The next weekend they flew in a smaller jet of his, heading southwest toward San Antonio. "This is in the Texas Hill Country. To me, it's a beautiful place," Jeff said.

Before long, when she looked below, she could see what he meant. They landed on a ranch runway and she was surprised by the rolling hills covered in grass, changed trees and wildflowers.

"This is different, Jeff," she said.

"You should see it in the spring. That's the prettiest time. The bluebonnets will be in bloom."

They crossed a clear, shallow river, driving on river rocks and a low-water road. The ranch house was sprawling, less flamboyant than his palatial mansion on his other ranch. "I'm beginning to see why you wanted this…."

"It has oil, cattle, horses. Herefords and Angus. This

is a thriving, productive ranch. I'll take you around tomorrow in the truck to look at it."

They spent the weekend and she wondered why he didn't move permanently. She liked it much better than his other ranch. On the flight back Sunday night, she asked him.

"West Texas is home now. I like it the best. All the things you find odious about it are the reasons I like it and want to stay there. I'll visit the other place, but home is West Texas."

"I don't know how you can feel that way," she said, unable to understand his preference, but then she understood little about Jeff.

Eight

Holly wondered how many more ways Jeff would change her life. A rodeo was one of the last places she ever expected to be. While Jeff had a suite, he also had a box in front where he wanted her to sit since this was her first rodeo.

She was surprised how eager and excited he was.

Watching the saddle bronc riding, she couldn't imagine why anyone wanted to do any of the rides. She enjoyed the barrel racing, but that was the only activity that didn't scare her to watch. Finally, it was time for the bull riding. She closed her eyes after the first seconds of the first cowboy and bull out. She heard the gasp from the crowd and opened her eyes to see the cowboy sprawled on the sawdust and the bull stomping on him as the crowd gasped again.

The clowns lured the bull away and she expected medics to come out and carry the cowboy away on a stretcher. Instead men came out to get him and he rolled over. Holding his side with the men helping him, he got to his feet and the crowd applauded as they helped him off.

Finally the bull trotted through an open gate that a cowboy swung shut behind him.

She wanted to leave and she couldn't possibly watch Jeff. She saw the next cowboy as the bull lunged out of the chute, but then she had to close her eyes until she heard the applause from the crowd. As the clowns drew the bull's attention, the cowboy got to his feet. She couldn't imagine who was crazier, the clowns for risking their lives to keep the bulls away from the cowboys, or the cowboys for riding the bulls.

Then it was Jeff's turn. She knew he would want her to watch him. The chute finally opened and the big gray bull came plunging out, bucking and twisting while Jeff rode it. She was terrified for him, clutching the program in one hand until she crumpled it without realizing what she was doing. She held her breath, hating every second, cold with fear and closing her eyes, only to open them briefly because she was certain he would ask if she had watched.

The buzzer sounded; the crowd cheered and applauded as he jumped to the ground, flashing a grin her way and walking off to climb the fence and disappear. She let out her breath, realizing she had been frozen with fear. She cared what happened to him. Was she already in love with him and hadn't realized it? Had she been fooling herself about her feelings for him? Or had her dislike for the ranch clouded her thinking so much she hadn't seen that she was falling in love with him?

Whatever it was, she had cared with all her being what happened to him in that bull ride.

He suddenly appeared, sitting down beside her and pushing his hat to the back of his head, grinning at her. "How'd you like it? Are you having fun?"

She stared at him, still wanting to throw her arms around him and cry with relief that he was safe.

"How can you want to do that?" she asked.

"I take it you didn't like watching me," he said and his grin disappeared. She wondered whether she had disappointed him, but she didn't care. The whole rodeo seemed barbaric and terrifying to her.

"I was scared to pieces," she admitted, locking her hands tightly together so she wouldn't touch him. She wanted to grab his hands and hold them, hug him, just to feel him safe in her arms.

He gave her a quizzical look, reaching over to unlock her fingers. He looked up at her again. "You are scared, aren't you?" he asked her with surprise in his voice.

"Yes," she hissed, angry that he would risk his life so foolishly.

"I'm fine. It's not that dangerous. Well, maybe it is, but I was doing what I like to do. I like the competition, the knowledge I can do it. It gets the adrenaline going and you're thankful to be alive. When I win, I feel great."

"Have you ever been hurt?"

"Sure. But I mended and got over it. Broken bones heal."

She ran her hand over her eyes, certain she would never understand him or like what he liked.

"C'mon. You're not watching, anyway."

She got up and left with him, walking into the hallway that had a few people standing around or coming and going. She could hear the announcer, smell the hay and horses and hear people talking.

Jeff pulled her into his arms and she couldn't keep from hugging him hard. "I was so scared for you," she said, trying to get a grip on her emotions and not let him see that she was worried. "Jeff, this is a ghastly sport."

He shook his head. "No, it's not. It's stuff cowboys do anyway. It's part of our lives to ride and rope. Well, riding bulls isn't, but the other events are."

She released him and stepped back. "Sorry, I just wasn't ready for this. That first cowboy got hurt...."

"He walked out of there on his own. He's okay. Had a broken rib or two."

"It just seems a ridiculous sport. Sorry, it's not for me."

"Hon, I think I hear the announcer saying my name. I may have won. Come with me—let's go see."

She nodded, still shocked over her own discoveries about herself and her feelings for him. She hoped that he didn't have an inkling how upset she had been over his ride.

She didn't want to be in love with him. His life was as foreign to her as someone from another planet. This was not the man she wanted to love.

Back when Noah had been single, she had never been drawn to him physically, yet Jeff was his identical twin. Noah was the twin she resembled. Noah was professional, wound up in business, loved opera, liked the things she did—yet she had never once been attracted to him. What was this wild chemistry that she had with Jeff from the first moment that she had looked into eyes identical to his brother's?

She watched Jeff talking and laughing with the

officials as he collected his winnings. His hat was pushed back on his head and he looked as if he had done nothing the entire evening. She would never understand his lifestyle or his love of it.

On the drive home she was quiet in the face of his excitement. The minute they stepped into the house, she turned to pull him close, standing on tiptoe to kiss him, thankful he had survived the evening.

His arms went around her and he kissed her.

She wanted him desperately, wanted to make love and reaffirm that he was his usual self. Clothes were shed across the kitchen and they made love on a leather sofa in the den.

He shifted to hold her against him as they lay on their sides. "What brought that on? It couldn't have been a high from the rodeo."

"I was so scared for you," she admitted. "I just wanted to know you're safe. I cannot begin to imagine why you like to ride. You don't need the money."

"I told you why. It's a challenge."

When she shuddered, he frowned. "Stop worrying. If I see it as fun and exciting, you shouldn't be uptight about it. Besides, a year from now, we'll part and it won't matter at all to you. Look at it that way. Frankly, I'm flattered you were concerned."

She felt the blush burn her cheeks and looked away from smoky eyes that might see too much. She hadn't wanted to let him know how scared she had been, but she couldn't help her reactions and it was too late now.

"You're right, of course," she replied, trying to keep her voice light and be more cheerful. "I just don't think I want to go to any more rodeos. I was anxious whether you were hurt or not, but I was scared for each of those riders."

"Aw, shucks," he drawled. "Here I thought all that distress was over me."

"A lot of it was," she said lightly, hoping he had no inkling how consumed by fear she had been.

"Let's shower and get in bed," he said, scooting around to sit and pull her into his arms. He stood and headed toward the stairs.

"Jeff, put me down. Let's gather our clothes. I don't want the staff to come in the morning and find my underwear strung across the kitchen."

He chuckled and set her on her feet. "We're newly-weds, I don't think Marc would fall out with shock."

"I don't care. I'm getting our clothes."

"I'll get mine," he said, grabbing up his and then turning to watch her. When she realized what he was doing, she yanked her clothes in front of her.

"You're embarrassing me. Stop looking."

"The view is spectacular. I'm not about to stop. Have I ever told you that you're a beautiful woman?"

"As a matter of fact, yes, you have," she said, grabbing the last of her clothes, trying to cover herself and hurrying to him. "You are a rogue!"

"Rogue? What century did you get that out of? I've never been called that before," he said, grinning as he draped his arm around her and they headed toward their bedroom.

Before falling asleep, they made love again. It was three in the morning before she drifted to sleep, hoping she didn't dream about the rodeo.

After breakfast Jeff left to take care of morning ranch chores since it was the weekend. He was still amazed by her reaction to the rodeo from the past night. He had hoped she would like it, but wasn't surprised that she had not enjoyed it. What astonished him, and he still was mulling it over, was her fear for his safety. When had she gotten so she cared?

He had been shocked when he joined her in their box and she had grabbed him, holding his hand tightly. Her knuckles had been white when she locked her hands together in her lap. She had been terrified for him and he had never expected any such reaction from her. He couldn't imagine her falling in love with him. She hated everything about his lifestyle. Or was she changing?

They still talked about when the marriage would be over and they would part. She seemed okay at the prospect. Actually eager, most of the time.

He acknowledged it was the best relationship he'd had, but he'd often felt that way in the past about someone and then when it was over, he could say goodbye easily and move on. He expected to do the same with Holly. Heaven help him if he ever did fall in love with her, because she didn't like one thing about his lifestyle.

People changed and maybe she was changing, a little bit at a time. He rubbed the back of his neck. He was still set on getting out of this marriage at the end of the year and hoped she felt the same. He didn't want to hurt her.

That night as he sat with Holly on the patio after dinner, he held her hand, rubbing her smooth skin lightly with his thumb. "Would you like your own horse and to go riding some mornings with me? I can get you a gentle mare. It's beautiful out there, Holly, watching the sunrise and seeing the mist on the ponds some mornings."

"No, thank you, Jeff. I did that as a child and didn't find any great thrill in it. You go enjoy your rides. I'll pass."

"You don't know until you try."

"Like the rodeo? I think not. Too dangerous for me." She sighed. "How is there any hope of meeting and sharing anything except…" She clamped her mouth closed.

Amused, he watched her face flush. "Except—finish your sentence."

"You know what I was about to say."

"Sure do. The one place where we have the same interests big-time—in bed. The sex is beyond my wildest dreams."

"Most amazing, considering everything else," she said, sounding more annoyed by the minute. "Actually, there have been moments in business when we've agreed and wanted the same thing. You can be professional and quite successful when you put your mind to it."

He chuckled. "I can hear your *but* without you having to say it. Most of the time you don't think I'm any of those things when it comes to work and Brand Enterprises."

"Maybe not," she admitted, blushing again. "You're very laid-back and unbusinesslike a lot of the time, but when you have to, you rise to the occasion."

"Come here," he said, wanting her, thinking about being in bed with her. He tugged her wrist and stood to pick her up, carrying her into the house. "I'm ready to *rise to the occasion* as you said. We're missing out on some fun and I don't intend to do so." He walked into the first bedroom on the ground floor and set her on her feet to pull her into his arms.

* * *

The ringing of the phone woke her and she opened her eyes in darkness, momentarily disoriented. Jeff reached out to pick up the phone and she glanced at the clock to see it was three in the morning.

His hello was sleep-filled, sounding slightly gruff. In seconds he sat up and his voice changed, becoming alert, and she realized something had happened.

"Where is he? I'll be right there. I'll take the plane," he said, tossing aside the sheet. A ceiling fan turned lazily overhead. She reached for her nightgown to pull it on and stood as he hung up the phone.

"What's happened?" she asked.

Nine

"It's Dad. He's had another heart attack and he's in the hospital. This just happened about an hour ago. Noah called as soon as he could get a chance. I'm flying to Dallas."

"I'll go with you."

"I'll be glad to have you, but you don't have to."

She was already headed out of the room. "I'll be ready as quickly as I can," she tossed back as she rushed to shower and dress.

Within the hour they were in his jet, flying east toward Dallas. She reached over to squeeze his hand. "I'm sorry, Jeff. I hope everything is okay when we arrive and that he's better."

"Thanks," he said, holding her hand. "He's made it through these twice before."

When they reached the hospital, Jeff hugged his mother, who turned to hug Holly. "Thank you for coming with Jeff, Holly. This is so awful," she said, dabbing at her eyes. Noah greeted her and then turned to talk to Jeff and she stepped away.

It was dawn when Jeff finally joined her. "The prognosis looks good. Dad is being monitored. We have a private nurse with him so he has constant attention. Let's get out of here. I've told Mom I'll see her later. She has a room near here. Noah is going to take her there. I offered to, but he told me to take you and get some sleep. I can relieve him later today. Let's go to your condo."

Holly left with him to go to her condo. While Jeff went to the hospital the next day, she went to the Dallas office.

That night she met Jeff for dinner. "I've missed you today," he said after walking up to her to kiss her cheek. "Dad's better," he said as soon as the waiter had their drink order and they were alone. "They think he can go home by the end of the week, so we can go back to the ranch."

She hoped she hid her disappointment over leaving Dallas, though she was happy to hear Mr. Brand was improving. She had enjoyed the day at the office, feeling as if she had gotten more accomplished than she ever did at Jeff's ranch.

"I'm glad he's better, Jeff."

"His doctor told him to step down as chairman of the board. He has to cut all ties with the office and retire totally. I don't know how that will sit with him, but Noah and Mom are urging him to follow the doctor's orders. I'm sure Uncle Shel has talked to him about it, too."

"They'll probably make Noah chairman of the board."

"I'm sure and he can handle it. He's still got to fill the COO spot." Their waiter poured ice water and then opened a bottle of wine and offered it to Jeff for his approval.

As soon as they were alone again, she sipped her wine. His cell beeped and he pulled it out of his pocket to answer. He spoke softly and she didn't listen to his conversation, but noticed his frown. "Your dad?" she asked when he replaced the phone in his pocket.

"No. That was Deke at the ranch. We've got something killing livestock. If they haven't found it by the time I get home, I'll help look."

"What do you mean *something?*"

"Could be a big cat passing through. I can't imagine a coyote getting anything big. They haven't been able to tell from the tracks yet."

"I'll never understand the life you love. Are we returning to the ranch tonight?"

"No. It's late. We'll stay and I'll see how things are tomorrow. Go ahead and go to the office if you want. We can leave after work unless there's a reason to stay longer."

"That's great," she replied and he smiled.

"You're always happier here, aren't you?"

"Yes. Just as you are always happier at the ranch," she answered and he nodded. "I catch up on everything happening at the office, keep my contacts. I just feel I get twice as much accomplished."

"At the moment, I'm just enjoying tonight and being alone with you. I don't care where we are, although I'm glad I don't have to drive back to the ranch tonight. I have other plans and I don't want to wait."

Her heartbeat quickened because she knew he wanted to make love and she was ready, losing all interest in dinner. "Maybe we could get these dinners to go."

Something flickered in the depths of his eyes as

he smiled at her. "That's the best idea I've heard all week."

Shortly, dinners were brought to them boxed and in a sack. Jeff paid their bill, tipped the waiter and they left, heading for their cars to meet at her condo.

When they stepped inside, she took the sack from him. "These go into the refrigerator first. We're not letting two delicious dinners spoil because we left them out." She carried them to the kitchen to unpack them. As she did, Jeff came up behind her, slipping his arms around her waist while he nuzzled her neck.

"Jeff, just wait!" she said, but her words were breathless. She inhaled deeply and tried to concentrate on putting the boxes in the refrigerator, struggled to ignore Jeff and, unable to at all, finally jammed everything into the fridge and slammed the door, turning into Jeff's arms.

"You're terrible. You wouldn't let me get that done in peace."

"I barely did anything," he whispered, kissing her throat and moving up to her ear.

She wrapped her arms around him, stood on tiptoe and kissed him. His arms banded her waist tightly and he leaned over to kiss her. "I've missed you all day," he said gruffly.

Her heart pounded as she held him tightly. In minutes he picked her up to carry her to bed.

She returned to the office the next day while Jeff went to the hospital. If only he liked Dallas and working in the city.

If all went well at the hospital, she expected to see Noah later today. She thought about the COO opening and felt certain Noah would at least offer it to Jeff.

Jeff's record so far would justify it if Noah did offer. Would he be able to turn it down? She couldn't see how anyone could turn down the chance for COO at Brand Enterprises.

She thought about Jeff and their lovemaking the night before, getting lost in daydreams until one realization brought her back to sharp focus. She was in love with Jeff. How deeply she didn't know, suspecting each day together forged stronger bonds.

She couldn't imagine that he felt anything serious in return. He was too wrapped up in his own world with far too many women waiting in the wings. Women who were like him and loved his boots and big hats and cowboy lifestyle. Women who'd love the gift of a horse from him and would ride with him whenever possible.

In spite of the differences, she was in love. How could she do this twice? It would be another ill-fated relationship with Jeff.

She couldn't imagine ever forgetting Jeff. He was larger than life, forceful and dynamic in spite of his easygoing manner. He was the negotiator and closer that Noah had promised. Now she understood why Noah had fought to get Jeff on board and why Noah had made so many concessions for him. It had been worth it to the company. As great as Jeff was in business, she couldn't fathom his dislike of it. But then she understood little about him. She simply had fallen in love with him. She closed her eyes, remembering the night before, recalling each kiss, each caress.

The phone rang, ending her reverie.

Midafternoon when Noah arrived at the office, she learned that his father would be released to go home

Friday. Noah didn't mention any official changes and she didn't want to ask.

Jeff and she flew home the next morning.

At the ranch, she watched him load a rifle and a pistol. "How many of you will hunt that cat?"

"Probably three of us."

"Three? That's not enough. You won't get out of the truck, will you?" She knew she was quizzing him too much.

He looked at her, pausing in what he was doing. "I won't be in a truck," he said. "A truck will make too much noise. I'll be on a horse. That's a natural sound to a cat."

"A horse won't give you any protection," she blurted, more worried than ever. "Jeff, you'll be vulnerable on a horse."

He waved a rifle at her. "That's what this is for. Stop worrying. I won't take unnecessary chances."

"Why do you always have to do all these dangerous things?"

He looked up again, narrowing his eyes, and she blushed, realizing how she sounded. She was twisting her fingers together and she put her hands behind her back quickly.

He tilted his head to one side. "You *care.* A month ago you wouldn't have cared if I'd gone out on foot to hunt down three cats and a grizzly. You would have cheerfully waved goodbye." He placed his rifle carefully on a nearby table alongside his pistol. Her heart drummed as he turned to approach her, his gray eyes unreadable.

"I guess I do care, but we've had some intimate moments. That changes a relationship that was as remote as could be to something close." Her face was hot, she was nervous, and growing more so by the second.

He placed his hands on her shoulders. "You don't need to explain. I'm flattered and glad we're not at swords' points, which we almost were in the beginning."

"We're married, Jeff. It may be a fake marriage, but it throws us together constantly and in many different ways. That alone engenders some caring. I can't imagine you feel about me the way you did that first afternoon."

"No, I don't," he replied somberly. He ran his hands back and forth on her shoulders. "I'm glad there's caring between us. It makes life together easier. I know we won't fall in love, but caring is good, Holly."

"I'll worry about you out there on a horse. What protection will that be? And you'll split up, so you'll be on your own. You'll just be a big target."

He tilted up her chin. "Stop worrying. I won't take unnecessary chances. I've done this before. I'll be careful and the critter will be scared of me. I'm not going to get attacked."

"You don't know that. You live the most primitive life."

He smiled. "Hardly," he remarked, pulling her close to kiss her. She held him tightly, kissing him, frustrated that he would shrug off any danger. He released her slightly to look down at her. "You make me want to chuck going and do something else."

"Go on," she snapped, her anger growing. "I don't understand your lifestyle, your love of risk and danger. How we have this wild chemistry between us, I'll never know," she blurted and then wished she could take back her words.

"I'll never know, either," he replied in a solemn

tone. "But we sure as hell have it, something I've never had before," he added, rubbing her jaw lightly with his finger. "The old saying is right, opposites attract. We couldn't be more opposite."

"No, we couldn't. Go on, kill your critter before he eats you," she said, pulling away from Jeff before he saw too much or she said something to reveal more of her feelings for him.

She heard his chuckle as she left. She hurried to her room to shut herself away from him, but in minutes she left to walk across the hall to an empty suite. She walked to the window where she could see the corral. Four men milled around minding horses with rifles in holsters. She watched Jeff mount a black horse that pranced nervously while Jeff talked to the men. One cowboy climbed into a truck and she hoped he would be close at hand wherever the others went.

Why, oh, why had she fallen in love with him? He was too many things she didn't like. She knew he had a lot of qualities she did like, though, enough to outweigh the others easily. She loved him and was afraid for him and knew it was ridiculous to worry. No one could stop him from doing anything he was set on doing. He didn't view danger in the same manner she did. He thrived on it and was a daredevil risk-taker deluxe.

She had to shrug away her fear for him. Either that or worry herself sick and make a fool of herself with him. He would soon realize she was in love with him in that case.

She tried to keep busy and go on with a normal workday and live life as if Jeff's absence didn't matter.

Knowing she was failing to forget about him just annoyed her more. She glanced often at the clock and caught herself repeatedly worrying about what he was doing.

At nightfall when she returned to his mansion, Holly was glad to see Marc still there until she discovered Jeff had asked him to stay because she was unhappy with him for tracking the cat that had been killing livestock.

"Don't worry, Mrs. Brand. Mr. Jeff knows how to take care of himself. He'll come home with that cat, you can bank on it. And he'll be all right. He's a clever man and sure of what he's doing. He's also a crack shot," the tall, dark-haired cook said.

"He could be all of that and something could still happen to surprise him," Holly said, finding it a relief to say it aloud.

"He knows what he is doing. I can assure you of that. I've worked for him eight years now. He knows how to take care of himself."

"It's hard not to worry. I'm a city person and I just can't imagine any of this—it'll be dark soon. The worst thing I've had to get off my property were little ants. I'm accustomed to dealing with city problems, work problems, but not something that might want to kill me."

"As I said, he can take care of himself. He'll come home with the carcass. Don't you worry."

Holly shuddered and left the kitchen.

The night turned out to be one of the longest of her life. She watched the clock, and with each passing hour, she grew edgier and more afraid for him. She realized she was as frightened for him as she had been at the rodeo.

When the phone rang, she pounced on it, holding

her breath and then letting it out in relief as Jeff's voice came over the line.

"Hi, love," he said. "How's it going?"

"I'm worrying about you. Thank goodness you called. When will you be home?" She couldn't keep from asking, knowing she should sound blasé. She didn't want him to realize she was in love with him. She had done that once before with her ex-fiancé and he trampled her feelings. Here she was doing the same thing all over again.

"Probably not tonight. Go on to sleep. And don't worry. We'll get that cat if he's still in the area. I miss being with you," Jeff said, his voice becoming husky.

"I'm glad you do," she replied. "I'm in bed, missing you, wanting your arms around me."

He groaned. "That's torment, Holly," he said.

"Then come home to me. Sleep here tonight."

"I can't, but don't think I wouldn't prefer to. I'll call if anything changes. 'Night, love," he said softly and then he was gone.

"Jeff Brand, you're a barbaric cowboy. I hate your wild lifestyle," she said to the empty room, knowing it was going to hurt to leave him. What would happen when Noah offered him the COO position? She was certain Noah would.

It was four in the morning when the phone disturbed her. She stirred and answered, coming awake swiftly when she glanced at the time. She held her breath and then let it out when she heard Jeff's exuberant voice. "We got him and we're home, Holly. I wanted to call before I walked in on you. We're at the barn and you can see the cat tomorrow."

"I think I can wait forever to see it," she replied, her

pulse racing because he was home safe and would soon be in her arms.

She replaced the phone, sitting up in bed and turning on one small lamp on a table.

She heard his boots on the hardwood floor before he even opened her door and entered. He crossed the room to her as she dashed to meet him. He caught her up and spun her around. He smelled of sweat and leather and aftershave. She was overjoyed to be in his arms and to have him safely home.

"Heavens, Jeff, you do worry one," she whispered before kissing him and ending his reply.

Much later, she lay in his arms while he talked about the events of the night. "It's a mountain lion. I'll show it to you later."

She didn't want to see the animal, but thought she should look to please Jeff. "The main thing is, you're back home."

He rolled her over to kiss her, causing her to forget about the night.

Later, standing at the corral, she watched the men take pictures, and her dismay returned. It was an enormous cat—as big as lions she had seen in zoos. From what the men were saying, Jeff had killed it—one more accomplishment that he would relish and that was appalling to her.

When she entered Brand headquarters Monday morning, relief filled her to be back in Dallas, even if only for the day. The orderliness and civilization of the office, the people around her, the bustle of the city, all of it was more welcome than usual.

Knowing Jeff's penchant for doing what he wanted to do with stubborn tenacity and that particular Brand drive he shared with Noah, she wondered whether Knox would step down and fully retire, or continue to risk his life and stay on as chairman of the board. She suspected he might well just stay. She glanced at the calendar on her desk. If she was already in love with Jeff, after a year in this marriage how strongly would she care about him?

Relieved to be out of Dallas, Jeff entered his office at the ranch Tuesday. He saw he had a call from Noah and he returned it, listening to Noah tell him he was on the way to the ranch and should arrive in another half hour.

Trepidation filled Jeff as he went to Holly's office. She looked up from her desk. They'd had breakfast together and made love earlier this morning, but he wanted to close the office door and go take her in his arms and kiss her right now. He suspected she wouldn't allow any such thing at the office with the secretaries due to arrive at any minute.

She looked up expectantly. "You don't look happy. What's going on?"

"Noah just called. He'll be here in about half an hour. He wants to talk to me about business."

"I can make a guess."

"No telling and no need guessing. I'll know before the hour is up."

The secretaries arrived and Jeff told them about Noah. Shortly afterward, Noah was ushered into Jeff's office. Looking as professional as ever, he was in a navy suit with a matching tie.

"To what do I owe this visit? When you come to the ranch, you're always on a mission."

"You're right," Noah said, smiling. "Jeff, Dad wanted

to see me last night. Faith, Erin and I went for dinner and afterward, Dad got me off alone. He's agreed to retire completely."

"That's good news because it's what he should do."

"Uncle Shelby is at the house now to see him, probably congratulating him and making Dad mad that he stepped down."

Jeff chuckled, a small laugh that faded quickly because he knew Noah hadn't touched on the reason for his visit. Jeff dreaded hearing what it might be. "I suspect I better wait for the other shoe to drop. And…"

"The board will have to approve, but I'll be offered CEO."

"Congratulations, Noah. It's coming earlier than you expected. You'll be great in that position."

"Thanks. You're right. It's what I've always wanted. You've done a great job, Jeff, which I knew you would. I've talked to Dad about this. I'm offering you COO. Think about it for several days before you give me an answer. Don't be too quick to say no."

Jeff closed his eyes briefly and shook his head. "I appreciate your offer absolutely."

"I drove all the way out here to talk to you about it. You'd have to work in Dallas, but you wouldn't have to give up your ranch. Jeff, you'd be damned good as COO. At least think about it and consider it. Is it such a strain working in Dallas now?"

"No," Jeff said, not wanting to tell Noah how relieved he always was to get back to the ranch, something he was certain Noah could never understand. "That's just one day a week. Five days a week is a whole different deal. That's the majority of the time."

"There would be all kinds of monetary rewards. Your

net worth would go a lot higher. Of course, I know the prestige and the contacts and all that sort of thing won't impress you."

"You've got that right," Jeff said. "I don't give a rat's ass for any of that."

"Sometimes I'm amazed that we're twins."

"I feel the same way. I'll think about it, Noah. I appreciate the offer, but the corporate world just isn't for me."

"That's difficult to fathom when you're good at it. I could understand if you were a failure or it was difficult for you, but it's not. You make it look easy. It probably is easier for you because you don't give a damn about the outcome when you make a deal."

"I want to make the deal, just like you do, but it isn't the same. It isn't as important. Now, riding in the rodeo—that's a whole different deal."

"Damn, I'll never understand."

"Neither does Holly," Jeff remarked and Noah raised an eyebrow.

"I'm sure that doesn't worry you one whit. No, she wouldn't. She's a city person through and through. Just think about it and see if you could stand to do it, even a few years. Five years—that's not a lot. You'd make a fortune."

"Noah, I appreciate this, but you can find good people easily. Executives who would jump at the chance. You told me you've been grooming Mason Cantrell for my position. Can't he do this instead?"

"I prefer you. I know I can find talent. Maybe I like working with you."

"Sure you do," Jeff joked. "We're competitive as hell when we're thrown together."

Noah smiled. "I still like working with you. Give it

some thought. I want you in that spot. Even two years would be good."

"Two years?" Jeff repeated, wondering how he could possibly stand the work for two years. One year was a prison sentence. "I promise I'll consider it, Noah, and I appreciate the offer."

"You've earned the offer."

"As long as you're here, you might as well stay for lunch. Holly will be glad to see you."

"Sure. I'll tell her to work on you about this, but then she probably has no power to move you to do anything, nor will she care."

"Might be," Jeff said lightly. "One thing, she'll think I've lost my wits if I turn you down. You know, Noah, you ought to offer the position to Holly. She could do it."

"I'm not thinking about that yet. I want you to consider it."

Jeff nodded. "Sure. Enough about that. Let's knock off and go to a place where you can get the best fried chicken in the southwest."

"You've got a deal."

To Jeff's relief, through lunch they relaxed and got away from business. Jeff enjoyed reminiscing with Noah and Holly seemed entertained. Before they were halfway through lunch, Holly and Noah began talking business as Jeff's mind wandered. He listened to them hash out new account details and talk about problems and successes, wondering how they could be wound up in Brand Enterprises 24/7. But it was what each one of them lived for.

He knew he'd never feel that way if he gave his life over to working for the family business. And he couldn't see accepting Noah's offer. The mere thought of it wasn't enticing.

"Holly, Dad is finally retiring completely. He's resigning as chairman of the board. There will be a formal announcement soon. They've had a board meeting and I'm the new CEO."

"Congratulations, Noah," Holly said. "I'm delighted for you and of course, you should be. Your father should feel he's left the company in competent hands."

"Thanks. I'm here because I want Jeff to accept my offer of the position of COO."

She turned wide green eyes on Jeff and he smiled. "I told Noah I'd think about it."

"Holly, use your influence on him to get him to accept. The company has already shown an increase in revenue because of Jeff," Noah urged.

"Jeff, congratulations to you on the offer," she said, her green eyes sparkling with excitement that he couldn't share. He looked at her mouth and wanted to get through lunch to be alone with her.

"That would be absolutely great if you and Noah would continue to work together," she said. He wondered if it had even remotely occurred to her that he would turn down Noah's offer.

"I'm flattered and I'm thinking about it, but I'm still a cowboy at heart. It would mean working in Dallas."

Noah laughed while Jeff noticed Holly did not, frowning slightly at him. As he looked into her eyes, he realized she had discerned his reluctance, something she probably had never thought of when Noah first announced the offer.

"You try to influence him, Holly," Noah said.

"I'm afraid I don't have that much influence on Jeff," she replied, still looking into his eyes. At the moment all he wanted to do was kiss that look off her face. It took an effort to pay attention to the talk about business.

"The new accounts are going to be a big asset," Noah said, and Jeff assumed he was talking about the ones he had acquired. Holly turned to Noah to ask about them and soon she and Noah were back discussing Brand business.

Finally Noah glanced at Jeff. "We're losing Jeff. I can see your eyes glazing over," Noah said. "You were right. This is the best chicken." He glanced at his watch. "I'd better head home."

It was another half hour before they told Noah good-bye. Jeff drove as they headed back to the ranch. Holly was quiet and rode in silence.

"Do you want to talk about Noah's offer?" Holly finally asked.

"If you'd like. I suspect you'd like to talk about it."

"When he announced it, I thought you'd accept it."

"It didn't occur to you that I'd turn him down or not jump at the offer, did it?" Jeff asked, mildly amused.

"No, it didn't. I still can't understand your love of the ranch and all it involves. It looks like ghastly work night and day. And where do you get a thrill out of it? You can't tell me you weren't excited and happy to get the Houston account," she said, turning slightly in the seat to look at him.

"First, the ranch—I love it. It's daily challenges, some new and unique, some routine. I need the wind in my face, the sun on me, the outdoors and my horses. I feel free, fortunate to be where I am and doing what I'm doing. Riding, roping, delivering a calf, fixing the truck, even fixing the fences—I always get a feeling of accomplishment. I get none of that with Brand Enterprises."

"That's just impossible, Jeff," she said in a tight voice. Whatever their physical relationship, they clearly remained poles apart in their life preferences, attitudes and ambitions.

"Let's get back to the ranch and back to things that we enjoy together," he said.

"This is an opportunity that half the world would be wild to get," she said, sounding annoyed.

"I know plenty of people would be happy to have this offer. I appreciate it, but it's not what I want. I didn't want to work in Dallas for this one year."

"Jeff," she said, closing her mouth and turning to look out the window. He knew she was unhappy with him and couldn't comprehend his attitude.

It was almost two in the afternoon when they reached the ranch. As they approached his house, instead of driving to the office, he parked at the back of his house.

"We ought to get back to the office. We've already lost time today," she said, sounding unhappy and impatient with him while he parked the car.

As he came around to open her door, she stepped out and slammed her door.

He took her arm. "We need to really talk, Holly. Let's go upstairs where we can be alone." He led her inside.

"Are we taking the day off?" she asked.

"We might be," he replied. "Let's go talk about Noah's offer. He told you to use your influence, so here's an opportunity."

"I don't have one shred of influence with you," she said.

"I disagree," he answered calmly, taking her arm as they walked through the back entry into the kitchen where Marc was pouring flour and milk into a bowl.

They both greeted him and Holly walked on through the room while Jeff stopped to talk. Shortly, he caught up with her. "Let's go to our bedroom. We can be alone and undisturbed there."

As soon as he closed the bedroom door, he pulled Holly close. She was stiff and resisted him, gazing at him with fire dancing in the depths of her green eyes.

"I'll never understand you. You're getting the offer of a lifetime and you don't want it."

"It just isn't what I want to do," he said. "I told Noah I'd think it over and I will. I know what I'm turning down and I know if I do, they will fill the spot just fine. Now while I'm considering it, there's something I'm far more interested in doing," he said, drawing her to him.

"We should get to the office. We're not alone here. You have staff all over your house."

Jeff leaned down to kiss her, his heart racing from desire that had been building for hours. "I want you," he whispered, kissing her lightly and then pulling her closer to kiss her more passionately.

She was stiff and unyielding for a few seconds and then she leaned closer. His arm tightened around her waist. She was soft, smelled sweet and he wanted to spend the rest of the day kissing and making love to her.

Kissing him, she wound her arms around his neck. He was aroused, wanting her and knowing no one would disturb them. He was also aware Holly was annoyed with him. As always, their physical attraction overcame their life preferences. In minutes she acted as if she had forgotten all dissension between them. To him, it wasn't that important.

He wanted her with a need that surprised him

because it seemed to continue growing instead of being satisfying or even diminishing.

As he kissed her, he unfastened the buttons of her black silk blouse and released her bra, cupping her breast, the softness filling his hand and raising his temperature. Desire escalated swiftly and the world beyond Holly ceased to exist.

Her softness was temptation, her kisses fire. He wanted to possess her, have her take him. Sex with her was spectacular each time, more than he had dreamed it would be and passion continued to heighten.

While he circled her taut bud with his thumb, he pushed her slacks away with his other hand, sliding his hand beneath her panties and caressing her intimately, light feathery touches that caused her to grasp him tightly and moan with pleasure. In turn, her responses heightened his own reactions.

He leaned down to kiss her breast, teasing her with his tongue, her hands moving over him increasing his need.

"Holly," he gasped, undoing his jeans and shoving away his briefs. She opened her eyes to gaze at him with desire blazing. He picked her up, braced himself against the wall. When he entered her warm softness, she cried out and bit his shoulder lightly, trailing kisses to his mouth.

Crying out again, she raked her hands over him as she climaxed and then his control was gone. He pumped furiously, holding her tightly while he reached his own climax.

Their breathing gradually returned to normal. "You're marvelous, love. You don't know what you do to me," he whispered, kissing her repeatedly. She was warm, pliant in his arms as she slid down to stand on her own.

"Jeff, you take advantage of me," she whispered and he leaned away to look at her.

"Do I?" he asked. She gazed up at him and smiled.

"Absolutely. You know I wasn't going to make love," she answered while she caressed him and kissed his chest lightly.

He picked her up. "We'll shower."

"This doesn't change how I feel about Noah's offer. I just don't understand how you can turn it down."

"I told him I'd think about it and I will, but I can't imagine changing my mind. Holly, I have enough money to do as I please," he reminded her.

She nodded, but her slight frown remained. "Jeff, if you didn't bring in such huge accounts, I'd think you're hopeless. That's what's so frustrating. You're as good in the business world as your brother, and it's so easy for you. I don't understand how you can turn your back on it."

"I can with much happiness. I have a ranching business to run."

"We could argue all day."

"Instead, we'll shower and go back to work," he said, setting her on her feet. Would it be possible to shower with her and not get aroused again?

Ten

It was three o'clock before they returned to the office and Holly felt her cheeks grow pink as she walked in to the knowing smiles of both secretaries. It was a relief to reach the privacy of her own office. Even with her door left open, she was alone and the afternoon with all its surprises replayed in her thoughts.

Noah's news of his dad's full retirement and then the offer to Jeff had stunned her. For one brief moment she had a flash of joy and excitement over Jeff moving to Dallas. Even as well as she already knew him, it hadn't occurred to her that anyone could turn down such an offer, not even Jeff.

She knew she was headed for disaster with him. In spite of all their differences, she was already in love with him. How that could happen still amazed her. Today had been typical. While she had been so annoyed with him, completely unable to understand his view, she had succumbed to his lovemaking—more than surrendering—loving him wildly in return and wanting him more than ever.

She rubbed her forehead. By the end of the year she would be so in love with him, she might never get over it.

With a loud sigh, she tried to turn her attention to work only to have her mind wander back to Jeff. How could anyone turn down COO of Brand Enterprises? It was the offer of a lifetime. A current of hot anger simmered all the time over his stubborn refusal to accept. And she knew he would refuse. He had argued with feeling today and she thought his promise to Noah to think it over was merely a token gesture.

How had she gotten in such a muddle, falling in love with a man she couldn't understand? It seemed as if her life were spinning totally out of her control.

She should have left Brand when Noah originally told her that she'd be working for Jeff.

Knowing he was burning bridges, Jeff walked into Noah's office and closed the door. Noah leaned back in his chair.

"Good morning. I can tell from the closed door that you've made up your mind about my offer."

"Yes, I have. I've given it thought. You know I appreciate it enormously."

Noah smiled. "I understand, Jeff. I always thought it was mostly Dad who ran you off, but it wasn't, was it?"

Jeff thought a moment before he answered. "No, it wasn't all him. I'm a cowboy and I love the ranch. I'm making a go of the ranch...."

"You're making more than a go of it," Noah said.

"I know you have money from Brand, from our trust, from oil and investments, but you run a damn profitable ranch."

"I'm turning you down. I just can't face returning."

"I'm not surprised, but I wanted you to have first chance at the job."

"I appreciate it, Noah."

Noah nodded. "You suggested Holly and I think you're right. She's capable and she'll take the job in a heartbeat. That's why I want to talk to you about it. She'll move right back to Dallas. If so, are you ready and willing for that? Will this tear up your bargain with Dad even if you do have the ranch?"

Jeff felt a lurch deep inside and it surprised him. "We'll keep up appearances of being married. That will keep Dad happy. It's okay with me," he answered lightly, but he knew, for once in his life, he wasn't answering Noah truthfully, something he had almost never done.

Noah's eyes narrowed and he stared at Jeff. "You're lying," he said.

Jeff inhaled. "I think you should offer the position to her and I know she'll take it without a pause. I think this is the right thing to do."

"You're getting mighty altruistic," Noah remarked.

"Just facing the facts. I know she'd love the position and she'll do a good job."

"I agree. Well, I'll be glad to have her back."

"We expected the marriage to end anyway."

"I can't understand how either of you could have gotten into such an agreement. Well, yes I can. You wanted the ranch and she wanted money and what you had to offer."

"Right." Jeff stood. "I'll get out of here and let

you talk to Holly. I'm happy for her. Again, Noah, thanks."

"I tried. I like working with you. When you go, tell Holly I'd like to see her. Let's all go to lunch together and celebrate if she accepts as quickly as you say she will."

He was surprised at how much he cared about seeing little of her from now on. And he knew she would be gone as quickly as she possibly could.

The idea hurt incredibly. He knocked lightly at her door, seeing her seated behind her desk. She looked up at him with wide eyes and for a moment he didn't want to tell her to go see Noah. He closed the door and she cocked her head to one side to look at him with obvious curiosity.

"Noah wants to see you," he said as he walked toward her.

"All right. Why the closed door to tell me that?"

Jeff walked around her desk without hesitation and pulled her up to kiss her. As he expected since they were in the Dallas office, she was resistant. To his satisfaction, as he persisted, her lips parted and she kissed him in return for a few moments. When she twisted away, he released her, looking at her intently and hurting because he knew their relationship would change as soon as Noah made the offer.

Would she still see him on weekends? She had to keep her part of the bargain, so their marriage would continue, even if in name only, for the year.

She misread his mood and reason for the kiss.

"You turned Noah down, didn't you?"

"Yes, I did. Sorry you're disappointed in what I did, but in the long run it won't matter to you. You'll be a lot happier this way."

Even though she merely nodded, he could see the disapproval in her expression. Jeff turned and went to his office and closed the door. His mind wasn't on Brand business and he didn't want to talk to anyone about business if he didn't have to. He hurt and he was going to miss Holly. He had always known this time with her would end, but he hadn't ever experienced a woman walking out on him. It had always been the other way around.

He knew he could pressure her to keep her agreement, one she had been paid to keep. He knew he'd see less of her than he did now.

He stood and walked to the window to look over Dallas, wishing he were at the ranch where he could do something physical to get his mind off Holly. The more he thought about her, the more he wanted to make love to her. He knew it would be tonight before he'd have an opportunity.

Holly sat in Noah's office, poised to take notes on whatever he wanted to discuss. "What did you want to see me about?"

"I suppose you know that Jeff turned down my offer."

"Yes. Noah, I tried to talk to him about it...."

Noah waved a hand. "Don't worry, Holly. I know Jeff. That isn't why I wanted to see you. I want to offer you the position of chief operating officer."

Shocked, she stared at him and then realized her mouth had dropped open. "Me? Noah, I'm stunned. And flattered and grateful. What about your board and Knox? They might not approve."

"I've already had private conversations with members of the board and they do approve. So did Dad. He thinks you'll commute and influence Jeff to work here longer. Everyone thinks you can do this job and do it well."

Excitement washed over her. "Noah, I'm ecstatic," she replied. She remembered Jeff's offer of setting her up in her own business. If she ever wanted to be in her own business, she would have enough money to do so later. For now, this was the chance of a lifetime as far as she was concerned.

"Of course I'll accept."

"I know I can count on you. You'll move back to Dallas, of course. You and Jeff can work out the terms of your paper marriage. I don't see why Jeff would care."

She couldn't wait to tell Jeff. "I'll talk to Jeff. Does he know you're making me the offer?"

"Yes. It was his idea."

Her second shock buffeted her, this time hurting. "It was Jeff's idea?" she asked, even though that was what Noah had just told her.

"Yes. He thought you'd be perfect for it and he's right."

She barely heard Noah's answer. If Jeff suggested her for it, it meant he didn't care at all about her moving back to Dallas and the two of them not seeing each other. For the second time in her life, she felt like such a chump with the man in her life. Her ex-fiancé had booted her out, suddenly announcing their engagement was over.

Now Jeff was essentially doing the same. She had known from the start that she shouldn't get emotionally involved with him, much less fall in love with him. She hurt and she had difficulty focusing on what Noah was saying to her.

"I'm sorry. This is so monumental," she said, feeling

her face flush with embarrassment. "I didn't hear what you just said."

"I know you're excited. I want to keep this quiet around the office until we work out some of the particulars. You'll have my office. I'm moving to Dad's. Take the day off so you and Jeff can discuss your future and go celebrate."

"Noah, thank you. Again, I'm so grateful for the opportunity."

"You'll do a great job. We'll get someone to replace you at the ranch with Jeff. You two will have to solve your marriage arrangements, but I know this won't place a hardship there."

"Not at all," she replied stiffly, hurt deeply that Jeff would want her out of his life, yet they were not compatible in so many areas. Why should she be surprised? "Noah, I'd like to stop working with Jeff at the ranch now. I work here on Mondays anyway, so I can just work all the time here in my old office."

He thought about it a moment. "I think that would work. People will wonder why, but I doubt if anyone will give it much thought. Sure. Go ahead. I know Jeff can get along. He may not like it, but he will."

Barely knowing what she was doing, she left Noah's office, went straight to her own, closed up and left for her condo.

She hurt all over and was angry with herself for getting so deeply involved with Jeff, for falling in love with him and for being a pushover all over again for a man who didn't love her.

Unfortunately, this time hurt more than the first time. She was much more in love and hurt so much worse. She drove home, trying to keep her mind on the road, yet failing, hearing other drivers honk at her. At last, she locked herself in her empty condo, fell into a chair and put her head into her hands to cry.

She cried until she felt she didn't have tears left and then began to think about the future and what she would do. She had to tell Jeff goodbye, which would be easy for him. She had to move her things from the ranch. And then it would be over. She would have to stay married for the rest of the year to fulfill her bargain, but it would be in name only.

He was here in the office today, so she washed her face, changed to slacks and a shirt and left for the ranch to move out while he was in Dallas.

She was making the last trip to the car with her things when Jeff drove up and climbed out of his car.

"Hey, what are you doing? You didn't tell me you were coming to the ranch," he said. As he neared, his smile faded. "What's wrong?"

"I suppose we need to talk now."

"It's hot out here. Let's go in where it's cool. We can have lemonade or iced tea or something," he suggested, taking her arm.

Her heart skipped from his touch and she wished she could be free of all feeling for him. Hurt squeezed her heart and she clamped her mouth closed.

In minutes he had lemonade for both of them and they entered the study where he closed the door and turned to face her.

"Thank you for suggesting me to Noah for COO, Jeff. He's offered me the position and I've accepted."

"That's what he told me," Jeff said quietly, approaching her. "Let's sit down."

She perched on the edge of a wing chair and he sat in one facing her. "It'll mean I'll live in Dallas now," she said, hurting, fighting her emotion and trying to avoid crying in front of him.

"If that's what you want," he replied and anger flashed in his gray eyes. "I know you're anxious to get away from here. You always have been."

"That's what I want. Noah said he would find someone else to work with you."

"I'm sorry to keep you in this marriage, even when it's just a paper agreement and merely for show, for a year, but that's the agreement we have and the only way I can retain the ranch."

"I know. I'm leaving immediately. I'll work in the Dallas office again even though they won't announce the promotion yet. Since I work there Mondays anyway, Noah thought it would be fine and I know you can get along."

"I won't like it without you, but sure, Holly. Whatever you want," he said.

She stood and he came to his feet instantly. She held out her hand. "It's been a lucrative and a pleasant experience," she said.

Something flickered in the depths of his smoky eyes and a muscle worked in his jaw. He took her hand to shake it.

"Yeah, Holly," he said stiffly. "Aw, hell," he snapped and stepped closer, wrapping his arms around her to kiss her hard and possessively.

Her heart thudded and she clung to him with all the pent-up hurt and need and knowledge this was the last kiss.

He held her tightly with one arm while his passionate kiss set her ablaze.

She stepped back, gasping for breath. "Jeff, let's stop. The sex has always been fun and exciting, but it's over.

I need to go. There never has been anything beyond sex between us, so why draw this out? This is goodbye."

"Okay, Holly," he replied.

She hurried across the room, picking up her purse. He caught up with her and walked her out.

"I'll see you in Dallas. You won't be back here, will you?"

"No, I won't," she said, hating the knot in her throat. To her horror, tears threatened and she took a deep breath and walked faster, climbing into her car swiftly.

"Goodbye, Jeff. Thanks for recommending me for the position."

He nodded, standing with his hands jammed into his pockets and looking grim. She drove away quickly, feeling hot tears stream down her cheeks. The tears blurred her vision. She hated crying, but she couldn't stop. She grabbed a tissue and wiped her eyes, looking in the rearview mirror at him standing in the road, staring after her.

"Goodbye," she whispered. "I love you," she said, hating that she had done the same dumb thing twice in her life.

Jeff watched her drive away. To his surprise, he was going to miss her badly. "Dammit, Noah," he said aloud, wishing the opening had never come up. He hated to lose Holly from his life.

He knew he'd get over her. He always had with the women in past relationships, but he hated it. He hurt more than he had thought possible. He walked back to the house to swim to get his mind off her. Returning to work would not do it. There was nothing about working for Brand that would get his mind off his problems.

* * *

Eagerness and anticipation increased as Jeff drove to Dallas the following Monday. He was having a celebratory lunch with Holly and Noah.

To his surprise, all weekend he had seen her everywhere he looked: at the office, at the house, at the pool.

At headquarters, he went straight to her office, knocking lightly on the door. She looked up with wide, startled eyes. His pulse drummed and he wanted to cross the room and take her into his arms.

Instead, he stepped inside to greet her casually. "How's everything?"

"Fine. They're going to announce my promotion tomorrow. It all worked out more quickly than Noah expected at first."

"Congratulations. Let me take you out tonight to celebrate."

"I'm sorry, I already have an engagement," she said. "Another night, Jeff."

He nodded, wanting her and knowing he had better get out of her office. "See you at lunch, Holly," he said, disappointment filling him. He left for his office, finding the place stifling. He wanted her and he hated trying to get his mind on business.

He knew Noah was just happy to have her back and have the COO position filled by someone competent, someone he could rely on. Noah wouldn't have a clue how Jeff felt about her. Sometimes all Noah could see was the business angle.

Lunch with her was even grimmer while at the same time, he liked being with her. She was bubblier than usual. The more time they were together, the more he wanted her.

She had ridden with Noah and Jeff had come alone. When he offered her a ride back with him, she politely declined and rode back again with Noah. It was clear she intended to shut him out of her life. On the drive back to the ranch that night, he knew he was going to hate the rest of the year he had to work for Noah. He missed Holly more each day.

Sitting on the patio and nursing the beer he had been drinking since sundown, Jeff stared at the blue sparkling pool and thought about Holly. He could no longer avoid the idea that he was deeply in love with her and hadn't faced his own feelings.

Was there a way to get her back? He knew there wasn't. She hated the ranch, loved her new position, loved her job and Dallas.

He should have accepted Noah's offer to keep working for Brand and have Holly in his life. Could he have given up the ranch for her? He was beginning to think he could. If he wanted to work in Dallas, Noah would find him a spot. He could do what he was doing now and work in the city. Would that give him a chance with her? He wondered about that. Could he bear to do that?

He thought that might be better than the hell he was going through now. If he couldn't stick with it, he would find out, but for now, it might put Holly back in his life.

Eleven

Holly dressed for work, pulling on a black suit—the dark color matched her mood. She missed Jeff—his companionship, the hot sex, his friendship, his fun ways, his charm, everything about him. She hurt more each day and had realized she was deeply in love with him, the kind of love that lasted a lifetime. All their differences no longer mattered.

Her job no longer mattered. She couldn't believe her own feelings, except she knew she dreaded going to work without him. She couldn't keep her mind on her job or pay attention in meetings. Even Noah had noticed and asked if she felt okay on more than one occasion.

Did Jeff miss her? Could he also be having second thoughts? She knew that was wishful thinking. He hadn't even called her. She both lived for Mondays and hated them. She loved being with him at the office, but he had suddenly turned completely professional with her, treating her with that polite manner he had always shown to the two secretaries who worked for him.

They were both gaga over him. She wondered whether he was taking one of them out now. The thought tormented her.

She even missed the quiet of the ranch. When had she become accustomed to the quiet out there? Or was it just that the quiet was a part of Jeff and she loved it along with him? She watched rodeos on television in hopes of catching a glimpse of him riding in one again because some shown were from Fort Worth and Mesquite.

Her phone rang and she raced to pick it up only to hear Jeff's voice. Her heart thudded as she clutched the phone tightly.

"Holly, I have to come to Dallas this afternoon to deliver a horse I've sold. I'd like to take you to dinner tonight and hear about the job. Can you go?"

"Yes, I can. Want me to meet you?" she asked, thinking how polite and distant they were being.

"I'll pick you up at your condo at half-past six. Can you make it home from work that early?"

"Of course," she said, "I'll be ready."

"I want to talk to you," he said.

"Fine," she replied, wondering what he had to talk to her about. He sounded solemn and she couldn't imagine what was on his mind.

"See you then," he said and was gone.

Her heartbeat skipped as she looked at herself in the mirror again, deciding to take off by five o'clock to go home to dress for dinner tonight.

All day she tried to guess why he had said he wanted to talk to her, going from wondering if he was going to say he missed her to telling her he had fallen in love with someone and wanted out of this paper marriage.

Except for the brief glimpses each Monday, she hadn't seen him now for three weeks. Three weeks of pure hell. Was he in love with someone else? Had he missed her?

She dressed in a deep blue, clinging sleeveless dress with a low-cut V-neck and a long straight skirt that was slit up one side to her thigh.

She left her hair down, falling freely around her face and she was ready twenty minutes early, wishing he would arrive before the appointed time.

When the doorbell rang, she hurried to the door to open it. In a charcoal suit, Jeff looked riveting. Her mouth went dry and she was certain he could hear her heart pound.

She stepped back with a smile. "Come in."

His smoky eyes had darkened, gazing intently at her as he entered and closed the door. Her heart seemed to slam against her ribs and all the things she had thought to say to him blew away like smoke in the wind.

"You look stunning," he said in a husky voice. "I've missed you."

As she stared at him, she couldn't think of what to say. All she wanted was to be in his arms. "I was wrong, Jeff," she whispered.

"So was I," he said, stepping forward to sweep her into his embrace and kiss her.

Her head spun while she held him tightly and returned his kiss passionately.

He stopped, gazing down at her. "I love you, Holly," he said gruffly and she thought she would faint with pleasure.

"Jeff, my love," she gasped. "I love you so and this job isn't worth it. You told Noah to hire me for it. I thought you wanted me out of your life."

"Never," he said, groaning. "I can't sleep, can't work, can't do anything." He leaned down to kiss her and end the conversation, finally picking her up in his arms to carry her to the bedroom to make love to her for the next two hours.

Later, he held her close in his arms. Naked, warm and satisfied, they lay with legs entwined, her head on his chest, listening to his heart.

"Holly," he said solemnly. "I miss you and I'll move back to Dallas and work here if I can get you back in my life." He shifted to look into her eyes. "I want to make this a real marriage. Will you marry me again? We can work something out because I just want you back in my life."

Surprised and overjoyed, she couldn't keep from crying with relief. "Jeff, yes, I will. I've even missed the ranch. You don't have to move to Dallas all the time. I just want you back in my life."

"I never told Noah to offer you COO to get rid of you. I knew you could do the job. I didn't stop to think about it taking you out of my life. I hadn't faced my own feelings. I hadn't realized how much I was in love. This is the first time in my life I've truly been in love."

She threw herself over him, kissing him and ending the conversation for another hour. Later as they sat eating a midnight dinner of peanut butter sandwiches in her small kitchen, Jeff said, "I brought you something." He left the room and returned to place a box in her hand.

When she opened the first of two boxes, she gasped as she stared at a huge emerald flanked by glittering diamonds. "Jeff, this is gorgeous."

"With this ring, I thee wed, truly and deeply in love forever," he said, slipping the ring on her finger.

She hugged him and then remembered the other box. She picked it up to open it, looking at a dazzling necklace of emeralds and diamonds that matched her ring.

"Jeff, this is spectacular. I'll be scared to wear it without a bodyguard."

"All right, I'll get you a bodyguard," he said, taking it and fastening it on her. He untied the sash to her robe and pushed it away. She grabbed at it.

"I'm not wearing anything.…" she yelped.

"You're wearing the necklace and ring I gave you. This is the way I like it."

She kissed him and their conversation was gone again until much later.

"Jeff, we can live at the ranch."

"I think I told you I'd live in Dallas."

"Maybe you can work here two days a week and perhaps Noah will agree to me working one day a week at the ranch. We might have to separate part of the week, but if I know you love me, I can get through it."

"Sounds like a plan to me. I just want you back in my life and back in my bed." He pulled her closer against him. "This is best, sweetie. You right here in my arms. My world is right again."

"I love you, Jeff. Everything about you. I'll even go to a rodeo again, although I'm not sure I can look when you ride."

He chuckled and held her tightly. "I'll give up bulls. I'll switch to calf roping. That's enough of a challenge. Differences are what makes life interesting. Take a couple of days off when you can and let's go off some-place where we can be to ourselves. I'll take you back to New York."

"That's fine with me. We're not going to leave the bedroom, anyway."

He smiled and brushed her hair away from her face. "You've got a deal, Mrs. Brand," he said.

Laughing, she hugged him, filled with joy.

Epilogue

One year later...

Knox Brand clinked a fork against a glass and raised his voice. "May I have your attention." He stood near the bar in the large family room of the Brand mansion.

All the family and close friends stopped talking, turning to give Knox their attention.

Holly was aware of Jeff moving close by her side and sliding his arm around her waist. She looked up at him and met his gaze, seeing the warmth in his eyes and the love that reflected what she felt.

Joy had bubbled in her all day and had increased tonight. She turned to give her attention to Knox.

"We're gathered here tonight to celebrate. Holly is retiring to await the arrival of our second grandchild—another little girl, I might add, and we want to congratulate her." He raised his glass as everyone applauded. She laughed at the hoopla being made over her retirement.

"We're delighted that Jeff and Holly are living in Dallas most of the time now. We want to thank her for all she did for Brand Enterprises, and wish her well in her new role as a mother."

Another round of applause filled the room and Jeff leaned down to kiss her lightly. "I'll second that," he said, touching her glass of sparkling water with his glass of wine.

"Folks," Noah said, causing another curtain of silence to fall over the guests. "I have to take the limelight from my dad and say a few words, too. Holly's done a marvelous job. We're lucky she fell in love with my brother and married into the Brand family. At work, we hate to lose her, but I understand and am just grateful for her talents and loyalty. We wish you and Jeff much happiness. Here's to you both and to another precious granddaughter for Mom and Dad and a little cousin for our Erin to play with." He raised his glass in a toast. People joined him and applauded.

In a minute Knox spoke up. "All right, everybody, enjoy yourselves. We have a spread outside and later there will be dancing. I think the kids are already in the pool or playing in the game room."

Holly waved her hand. "Knox," she said, stepping forward and linking her arms through Noah's and Knox's. "I want to thank everyone for coming tonight. Thank you for everything!"

For Holly, the evening was perfect. On the patio, a band played and couples danced. Kids were in the swimming pool and Noah held Erin in his arms. Holly looked at Noah's child, who had her mother's blond hair and her father's gray eyes and was beautiful. She wondered whether their baby would have red hair or black hair, green eyes or gray. Two more months and she would know.

"If you ever want to return, just let me know. And I don't know how you got Jeff to agree to stay on six more months," Noah said to Holly.

She smiled and looked at Jeff, who grinned and kept his arm around her waist, holding her close. "We'll be living in Dallas most of the time now because of the baby. Holly gave me all the logical reasons and said I owed it to you to give you at least six more months."

"Thank you again, Holly. I'm really going to miss you."

"Well, your loss is my gain," Jeff remarked. "I hope to see a lot more of my wife because you've heaped the work on her this past year."

"I didn't mind, Noah," she protested.

"Emilio," Jeff said to Faith's grandfather. "Come join us."

"All you young people? I will put a damper."

"Of course you won't," Faith said, taking his arm and smiling at him.

"Well, I'd like to hold my little great granddaughter," he said, holding out his arms, and Erin immediately reached for him. "I think someone is sleepy. Maybe we will go find a rocking chair," he said. "If all of you will excuse us."

He left and Noah draped his arm across Faith's shoulders. "These women, Jeff, how they've changed our lives... I must say, Holly has made you far more civilized."

Jeff laughed. "Look who's talking, Noah. Faith has softened that competitive nature of yours. You no longer have to win at all costs."

"I'll remind you of that the next contest we get into," Noah remarked dryly.

Holly was filled with happiness and love as she listened to the two brothers talk and knew there was some truth to what they said. They didn't seem as competitive and sharp with each other as they had before she married Jeff. And she knew for certain they had grown closer. She suspected when she and Jeff had their little girl, the two families would grow even closer.

Already, she counted Faith as one of her best friends. She still was amazed that Faith had married Noah, whose businesslike manner was a contrast to Faith's warm and fun-loving nature. Holly knew that people probably thought the same of her marriage to Jeff. They were total opposites, far more than Noah and Faith, yet she found Jeff more exciting every day she was with him. Her love knew no bounds and right now, she couldn't wait to be home alone with him tonight.

They mingled with the guests, talking to the Brands and Shelby, stopping to talk to Alexa and other friends. By the time the last guest left and Shelby had headed off to catch a plane, Holly was beginning to tire.

"I think we should call it a night. Holly's had a big day with her retirement party at work today, plus this party tonight. It's been a great evening," Jeff said.

She turned to Jeff's mother to thank her for the party. "What a wonderful party. I feel so welcome in this family. This is the first grandchild in my family and I have a feeling I may see more of my parents after our baby arrives."

"I know you will. Your mother asked me all sorts of questions about Erin," Monica Brand said, smiling at Holly. "I can't wait to have two little granddaughters.

Erin is an absolute delight. So much fun to buy clothes for and I won't have to referee fights."

Holly laughed. "Thanks again."

"Thanks, Mom," Jeff said, kissing his mother's cheek and hugging her. "It's been a great party and was nice for us."

Holly felt as if it were hours instead of a mere thirty minutes before they finally were alone in their Dallas home and in their bedroom where Jeff pulled her gently into his arms.

"I love you, Jeff Brand," she said happily.

"I love you, darlin'. And I'm glad you'll be home all the time now. I love you, Holly. You'll never know how much," he added, holding her gently as he kissed her.

"When she's three months old, we can move back to the ranch," Holly said.

"Shh. We'll figure that out when the time comes."

Holly wrapped her arms around his neck, feeling their baby between them. Joy flooded her. She knew she was the most fortunate woman in the world to have the love of a man like Jeff and soon she would have his baby. She kissed him, wanting to spend a lifetime showing him how much she loved him.

* * * * *

*Rancher Ramsey Westmoreland's temporary cook
is way too attractive for his liking.
Little does he know Chloe Burton came to his ranch
with another agenda entirely....*

That man across the street had to be, without a doubt, the most handsome man she'd ever seen.

Chloe Burton's pulse beat rhythmically as he stopped to talk to another man in front of a feed store. He was tall, dark and every inch of sexy—from his Stetson to the well-worn leather boots on his feet. And from the way his jeans and Western shirt fit his broad, muscular shoulders, it was quite obvious he had everything it took to separate the men from the boys. The combination was enough to corrupt any woman's mind and had her weakening even from a distance. Her body felt flushed. It was hot. Unsettled.

Over the past year the only male who had gotten her time and attention had been the e-mail. That was simply pathetic, especially since now she was practically drooling simply at the sight of a man. Even his stance—both hands in his jeans pockets, legs braced apart—was a pose she would carry to her dreams.

And he was smiling, evidently enjoying the conversation being exchanged. He had dimples, incredibly sexy dimples in not one but both cheeks.

"What are you staring at, Clo?"

Chloe nearly jumped. She'd forgotten she had a lunch date. She glanced over the table at her best friend from college, Lucia Conyers.

"Take a look at that man across the street in the blue shirt, Lucia. Will he not be perfect for Denver's first issue of *Simply Irresistible* or what?" Chloe asked with so much excitement she almost couldn't stand it.

She was the owner of *Simply Irresistible*, a magazine for today's up-and-coming woman. Their once-a-year Irresistible Man cover, which highlighted a man the magazine felt deserved the honor, had increased sales enough for Chloe to open a Denver office.

When Lucia didn't say anything but kept staring, Chloe's smile widened. "Well?"

Lucia glanced across the booth at her. "Since you asked, I'll tell you what I see. One of the Westmorelands—Ramsey Westmoreland. And yes, he'd be perfect for the cover, but he won't do it."

Chloe raised a brow. "He'd get paid for his services, of course."

Lucia laughed and shook her head. "Getting paid won't be the issue, Clo—Ramsey is one of the wealthiest sheep ranchers in this part of Colorado. But everyone knows what a private person he is. Trust me—he won't do it."

Chloe couldn't help but smile. The man was the epitome of what she was looking for in a magazine cover and she was determined that whatever it took, he would be it.

"Um, I don't like that look on your face, Chloe. I've seen it before and know exactly what it means."

She watched as Ramsey Westmoreland entered the store with a swagger that made her almost breathless. She *would* be seeing him again.

Look for Silhouette Desire's
HOT WESTMORELAND NIGHTS
by Brenda Jackson,
available March 9 wherever books are sold.

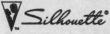

HARLEQUIN *Presents*

Two families torn apart by secrets and desire
are about to be reunited in

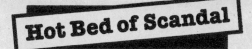

Hot Bed of Scandal

a sexy new duet by

Kelly Hunter

EXPOSED: MISBEHAVING WITH THE MAGNATE

#2905 Available March 2010

Gabriella Alexander returns to the French vineyard she
was banished from after being caught in flagrante with the
owner's son Lucien Duvalier—only to finish what they started!

REVEALED: A PRINCE AND A PREGNANCY

#2913 Available April 2010

Simone Duvalier wants Rafael Alexander and always has, but
they both get more than they bargained for when a night of
passion and a royal revelation rock their world!

www.eHarlequin.com

HP12905

REQUEST YOUR FREE BOOKS!

2 FREE NOVELS PLUS 2 FREE GIFTS!

Silhouette® *Desire*®

Passionate, Powerful, Provocative!

YES! Please send me 2 FREE Silhouette Desire® novels and my 2 FREE gifts (gifts are worth about $10). After receiving them, if I don't wish to receive any more books, I can return the shipping statement marked "cancel." If I don't cancel, I will receive 6 brand-new novels every month and be billed just $4.05 per book in the U.S. or $4.74 per book in Canada. That's a saving of almost 15% off the cover price! It's quite a bargain! Shipping and handling is just 50¢ per book in the U.S. and 75¢ per book in Canada.* I understand that accepting the 2 free books and gifts places me under no obligation to buy anything. I can always return a shipment and cancel at any time. Even if I never buy another book, the two free books and gifts are mine to keep forever.

225 SDN E39X   326 SDN E4AA

Name _____ (PLEASE PRINT)

Address _____ Apt. # _____

City _____ State/Prov. _____ Zip/Postal Code _____

Signature (if under 18, a parent or guardian must sign) _____

Mail to the Silhouette Reader Service:
IN U.S.A.: P.O. Box 1867, Buffalo, NY 14240-1867
IN CANADA: P.O. Box 609, Fort Erie, Ontario L2A 5X3

Not valid for current subscribers to Silhouette Desire books.

Want to try two free books from another line?
Call 1-800-873-8635 or visit www.morefreebooks.com.

* Terms and prices subject to change without notice. Prices do not include applicable taxes. N.Y. residents add applicable sales tax. Canadian residents will be charged applicable provincial taxes and GST. Offer not valid in Quebec. This offer is limited to one order per household. All orders subject to approval. Credit or debit balances in a customer's account(s) may be offset by any other outstanding balance owed by or to the customer. Please allow 4 to 6 weeks for delivery. Offer available while quantities last.

Your Privacy: Silhouette Books is committed to protecting your privacy. Our Privacy Policy is available online at www.eHarlequin.com or upon request from the Reader Service. From time to time we make our lists of customers available to reputable third parties who may have a product or service of interest to you. If you would prefer we not share your name and address, please check here. ☐

Help us get it right—We strive for accurate, respectful and relevant communications. To clarify or modify your communication preferences, visit us at www.ReaderService.com/consumerchoice.

SDES10

THE WESTMORELANDS

NEW YORK TIMES
bestselling author

BRENDA JACKSON

HOT WESTMORELAND NIGHTS

Ramsey Westmoreland knew better than to lust after the hired help. But Chloe, the new cook, was just so delectable. Though their affair was growing steamier, Chloe's motives became suspicious. And when he learned Chloe was carrying his child this Westmoreland Rancher had to choose between pride or duty.

Available March 2010 wherever books are sold.

Always Powerful, Passionate and Provocative.